Ember's Flame

a novel by

Serendipity

ISBN-13: 978-0-692-80677-7

Ember's Flame

For permission requests, please contact the author via the "Contact Me" page on the following website: www.authorserendipity.com.

Cover Design: Natalie Castillo

1st Editor: Anitra G. Louis

2nd Editor: Ashley Campbell

Proudly self-published through Divine Legacy Publishing, www.divinelegacypublishing.com

Dedication

To Dorothy, Frances, Melvin,
Dolores, Annie, Billy, and Karter.
The angels that look out for me and live on forever in my heart.

Acknowledgements

Lord, thank you for allowing me to accomplish my dream of writing a book.

Brooke, thank you for being my inspiration and motivation. Always remember, you can do anything you want. You are indeed my divine legacy. Mommy loves you to the moon and back.

Stan, thank you for loving me and taking this leap of faith with me. Your support and daddy day care skills make it possible for me to pursue my dream. You are my real life romantic hero, Woof. I love you, always.

Benita, thank you for being the type of mother that tells her daughter she can do anything. Your unconditional love, support, and encouragement have kept me afloat many times. You are amazing; I love you mommy.

Anitra, thank you for being the best SisterEditor I could ask for. Your pep talks and hilarity often keep me sane. You're truly one in a million. Love you.

ORDA, I love you all so much. I'm so blessed to have such an amazing group of women claim me. Don't ever disown me, okay?

Laura, Terrika, and Rosanna, you three are the bomb.com. I cannot thank you enough for having my back and being my soundboards. I guess I'll keep y'all.

Kirsten, thank you for lighting a fire under me. If not for you, this book would still be collecting dust on my hard drive.

Natalie, thank you so much for my awesome cover. **Kaylin,** thank you so much for the revision.

Thank you everyone. Thank you.

Chapter One

Ember Sinclair had to be setting a company record.

She was working late for the fifth night in a row, and the day before the Memorial Day holiday weekend. While she didn't mind staying after hours, even welcoming it at times, tonight was a different story. When she had gotten back from lunch she told herself that she would leave on time today. That was seven hours ago. Sitting at her desk for all that time without a break had taken its toll and her productivity had hit rock bottom. Even though she was supposed to be focused on a proposal for a client who could make or break her career in advertising, her mind kept wandering. Every time she would get herself back on track her eyes would move to her office door and she would be reminded of who was just down the hall in his own office.

Cole Bainbridge. Her boss. Forbidden territory. It was just something about the way he looked at her sometimes, so intently with his onyx eyes, she would swear he was looking into her very soul. But the rest of the time he was aloof, even distant, and she would convince herself that she had imagined his other look. At thirty-six, he was nine years her senior and the founding CEO of the advertising firm where she worked. He had a walk that oozed sexual confidence and it made his 6'1" frame seem even taller. She knew he was physically fit, though she had never seen him in anything but a business suit, because he often took his suit jacket off and she found herself watching the muscles play and flex under his shirt. Every suit he owned must have been tailored to his body; they fit too well to not be. His body moved with the ease and precision of a wild jungle cat. His skin looked like smooth, milk chocolate and at times she actually ached to taste it. Chocolate was, after all, her favorite flavor.

When she was first hired, she didn't have much contact with him past her interview besides performance reviews and the big promotion to Senior Executive she had gotten last year. But now, nearly five years later, she was working directly with him on the firm's client in the travel industry. Being in close contact with him for the last three months was wreaking havoc on her senses. She smelled his cologne even when he wasn't in the room. He high-fived her the other day and the touch sent tingles down her arm to her most sensitive areas. It seemed that she was perpetually horny. She went from being content to be celibate to painfully aware of her lack of a sex life.

She could desire him all she wanted, but having him was a different story. After witnessing the life changing drama that surrounds an unbalanced romance on more than one occasion, Ember would have none of that. Most recently she had a very good friend, Violet, go missing after a bad break up. There was speculation that Violet had killed herself, but Ember believed that Violet had decided to disappear when things became too hard. Either way, Violet had literally given up her life Ember wouldn't risk losing all that Violet had lost, no matter how much she may want Cole. Besides, she had a plan and wanted to open her own firm by the time she turned 30 and that left very little time for pursuing a man, forbidden or otherwise. The internal battle of wanting Cole but knowing that she shouldn't was almost as distracting as Cole himself.

Growing restless, Ember rose from her desk and walked to the large window on the right side of her office. She did this often, especially when she was having trouble focusing. There was something about watching the city move by that calmed her, and her window provided a spectacular view of downtown Raleigh. The sun had gone down and the area was alive with light coming from various restaurants and bars. Many people had already started their holiday celebrations and the streets were filled with loud, happy people.

She adjusted her vision and could see her reflection gazing back at her. Everything about her looked tired. Her usually smooth, caramel brown skin had small tired lines at the edges of her espresso colored eyes and, while her eyeliner was still firmly in place, her eye shadow was starting to fade into oblivion. There was a dull look resonating in her eyes, making her look half asleep. Her usually bouncy, curly black hair was pulled back and held up with a pencil. Her lips looked amazing though, as she had recently reapplied her favorite lip gloss. Sleep deprivation was no excuse for ashy lips; a girl had to have some pride. She looked down and saw that her stylish navy pinstripe skirt was hopelessly wrinkled from being worn for over twelve hours. She had long ago ditched her sweater, which she wore because the office was often kept ice cold, and her cream silk blouse looked worse for the wear. Her appearance matched her concentration level.

Tired or not, Ember had to get this proposal finished by the end of the first week of June and there was so much riding on it. She shook her head, forced herself back into work mode, and told herself that her lack of concentration had nothing to do with the man in the office down the hall. Ember turned away from the window and walked back to her desk, vowing to get her tasks done.

Her vow didn't last five minutes and before she knew it, she had twirled her chair around and was staring out of the window again. Again her mind drifted back to Cole. *Dammit.* She thought. *How am I ever going to get any work done with my mind wandering where it has no business going?* And the thoughts that she was having would shock even the most sexual person she knew, her best friend Cheyenne. Cheyenne prided herself on being sexually free and often bragged to Ember and their other best friend, Gabriella, about her sexual exploits.

Sex was on Ember's mind and she couldn't get it off . . . but she could get herself off and get her focus back. Realizing she was going to have to literally take matters into her own hands, Ember tilted her head back against her chair and began to let her imagination run wild. Although her mind didn't have time for men right now, her body disagreed and required regular attention. She was no prude and believed wholeheartedly in self-love. Closing her eyes she began to conjure up images of Cole, images she quite frequently summoned to aid in her self-love activities, or as she liked to call them, her ménage a mois. She envisioned Cole kissing her as she licked her lips and pretended her hand was his as she caressed her neck and slid it down into her blouse. Sliding her other hand up her thigh, she imagined it was Cole's fingertips caressing her. Sinking down ever so slightly in her chair, she raised her skirt just high enough to obtain what she wanted so badly to have Cole touch. As she fingered the edges of her navy and cream lace panties, she began to wonder what it would be like if Cole was really doing the touching instead of her. She was just about to slide her fingers inside her panties when her office phone rang. Startled, agitated and now even more sexually frustrated, she answered the phone on the third ring.

"Commercial Innovations, office of Ember Sinclair, how may I help you?" she growled out.

"Why are you still at work? You were supposed to be here twenty minutes ago! Gabriella and I have been calling your cell phone forever!" Cheyenne hollered in pure irritation.

"Oh, damn Chey! I'm working late again and my cell is on vibrate. I meant to call you but I just got so caught up in this research. I'm sorry."

"Are you serious? It's Memorial Day weekend! You can't possibly be working late again! You know . . . you've been spending a lot of time working late, it's kind of suspect. Did you finally get up the nerve to screw that sexy boss of yours? Now that's a man I would work late for. Hmmm . . . yes I would."

Slightly embarrassed at how close to right Cheyenne was, Ember defensively said, "Is sex the only thing on your mind...ever? I'm actually working. You know I don't mix business with pleasure so sleeping with Cole is out of the question."

"Hmmm, well, with your schedule it seems like the only way you can get some nookie is to get it at work."

"Funny, real funny. Now, if you are done probing into the inner workings of my non-existent sex life, I'm going to go and get some work done."

"What you need to do is go and get off with that fine boss of yours. How many times have you told me how sexy you think he is? He would be game, I know he would."

"Goodbye Cheyenne, I'll see you at the cookout tomorrow. Tell Gabriella I said sorry and I'll see her tomorrow." *Plus I was getting off when you interrupted me dammit,* she thought with aggravation.

"Okay, ignore me. You know I'm right. Later."

Hanging up the phone, Ember thought about going to see how Cole was coming along with his end of the work they were trying to complete tonight, but then thought better of it. Her conversation with Cheyenne had her even more sexually frustrated and thinking things she really shouldn't be thinking . . .

* * *

Placing his phone back in the receiver, Cole Bainbridge couldn't help but smile with pleasure. A long time ago, he had all afterhours phone calls routed so they would ring in both the specific office they were trying to contact and his office phone, since he often worked late and even slept at the office at times. That way he could handle any emergency situations that may occur overnight. Most of the time, the calls were slightly annoying non-emergencies that he quickly and easily handled; this time the call had been much more interesting. Swiveling his chair to face his open office door and the hallway separating his office from Ember's, Cole wondered what he should do with the information he had just acquired. He hadn't meant to eavesdrop, at least not at first. He had picked up the phone just a second after Ember, wondering why anyone would be calling the office at almost 7:30 on a Friday night at the start of a holiday weekend. When he heard Ember's friend asking why she was still at work, he felt bad. When they had discussed working late tonight she had not mentioned she was breaking plans to do so. Sometimes he forgot that work wasn't everyone's life like it was his. He should have hung up then, waited until she was finished with the call, and then went to tell her to go home and keep her holiday plans with her friends. Yet something had made him continue to listen to the phone call. Then he'd heard it: Ember wanted him. She wanted him enough to have discussed it with her friend.

He weighed his options: He could take the safe road, go into Ember's office and tell her to go home for the night, or he could finally satisfy this need to touch her that had been burning inside of him since the day she was hired over four years ago. He never acted on his impulses because he didn't have time for a sexual harassment suit—that was not something he even remotely needed in his life. He worked too hard to build his business to lose everything because he chose to make decisions with the wrong head. Things were different now, however, because he knew she wanted him. If they were different, then why was he weighing his options to begin with?

So many questions ran through his mind: How would she respond if he just walked in there and started doing all the things that had occupied his mind of late? Would it be fair to begin a sexual relationship with Ember, knowing she may want more and he couldn't give her that? After being pulled through the ringer by Denise, he knew that another committed relationship would be out of the question. Never again would he allow someone to be the focal point of his life. Not when he couldn't be sure if it was him or his money that made him so attractive. The saying "more money, more problems" certainly applied to his love life. Too many times he had found out that his bank account was what attracted women to him and what they were truly after; Denise had been the worst of the clan, and after her Cole knew he would be a bachelor for life. To him, women were now sexual companions, individuals to be respected but held at a distance.

Would Ember settle for being a companion or would she want more? Should he even pursue such a relationship with an employee? He had certainly taken notice of her when she was first hired, but their paths had rarely crossed until they began working on the Soul Escapes Cruiseline account together. During their most recent meeting he'd had to make a conscious effort to not stare at her the entire time. She was so poised and put together and he desired to see her come undone. He admired her look. She had a taste for vintage styles and her clothing always had a retro, soft, feminine feel to it. And she favored understated make up, except for the winged eyeliner she always wore. He was exposed to make up techniques and terminology by his younger sister Onyx, the Hollywood make up guru, and knew enough to know that Ember wore vintage make up styles and she wore them well. She was just all around beautiful. He sat and thought about the situation for a few more minutes, trying to make a decision. He felt like this was his now or never moment. Decision made, he rose from his desk and walked purposely out into the hallway.

Chapter Two

The knock on the door startled Ember back to reality.

"Miss Sinclair, may I come in?" Cole asked through the door.

"Yes, please come in," Ember said after clearing her throat and attempting to clear her mind. *Thank God I already fixed my clothes from my botched ménage a moi*, she thought as she watched Cole walk in. Tugging nervously on an escaped curl, she forced her attention on his eyes and away from his mouth.

"How are things coming along with the research for the proposal? Any strokes of genius?" Cole asked as he crossed the threshold of the door and sat down in one of the chairs facing her desk.

"A few. By the presentation in June we will be ready to wow Soul Escapes Cruiselines. The pictures of their ships that they sent over are beautiful. And the video of the interior was unbelievable. I mean, I did my research on the company when we first started courting them, but the pictures are just amazing. I can't imagine it will be too hard to sell people on a floating luxury mini city. I've never seen a cruise ship with a grocery store on board . . . or full kitchens in the larger cabins. That's an amazing thing to offer guests. And they sell organic foods and serve them in meals. Many people are making the switch to organic eating so that's an appealing selling point. It would certainly appeal to me. Oh, and I read that childcare is available. I've only seen that option on the theme park owned cruise lines. That's a great perk that will encourage entire families to book trips. Kids can play and parents can reconnect. The family-sized cabins are also a big plus. Two to three bedrooms with a common kitchen, dining, and living area is a really appealing offer. The hair salon is big, too. There are hair salons on a lot of the other cruiselines but most of the time the stylists don't know what to do with ethnic hair. The brochure for Soul Escapes says that they employ multiple stylists that specialize in ethnic hair. They even have an African hair braider. I know a lot of black women who hesitate to go on cruises because they don't want to walk around looking crazy because the sea air has demolished their hair. One of my best friends, Gabriella, is an amazing stylist and she would kill to work on a cruise ship." Ember was unsure if it was her lack of sleep or the scent of his cologne that had just reached her nose but she was starting to ramble and it was time to get him out of her office. "Was there anything you needed from me, Mr. Bainbridge?"

"I think you've been here long enough tonight, it's unfair of me to expect you to keep the same grueling hours I keep. It is a holiday after all. Go home, relax, and enjoy the holiday." *Before I renig on my decision to not pursue you*, he thought.

There he was doing it again; looking at her so intently she would swear he was about to pounce. "I've just got a few more things to look over and then I'll head out, shouldn't take me more than a few hours. I'll be gone by ten at the latest."

Looking at his watch, he saw that it was only 7:47, which meant she planned on being here for another two hours and thirteen minutes. He didn't have that much restraint. Armed with the knowledge that she wanted him, even ten more minutes alone with her would test his self-discipline. He had to come up with something fast.

"Well, I'm actually about to head out myself. I don't mind

you working late when I'm here but I'm not sure it's safe for you to be here by yourself at such a late hour. I know you've been here late the last few days but I was here with you," he said.

"I thought you said in our afternoon meeting that you planned on spending the night here and sleeping on the couch in your office when you finished for the night. Remember we all tried to talk you out of doing such a thing when you have a nice, comfy bed at home? You've changed your mind?"

Shit, he had said that hadn't he? "Well, I was just heading out to grab some dinner and bring it back here. I don't want to leave you here alone for any amount of time. I don't think it's safe to do that."

"I'm actually hungry too, Mr. Bainbridge. It's not too late, would you mind ordering something to be delivered here? That way I can stay, you can get more work done, and we both can eat?" She watched him stammer for an answer and realized he must have had a dinner date. Maybe he even planned to bring his date back to the office for a little holiday coitus. He certainly couldn't do that with her here. Suddenly disturbed by her assumption that he had a date, she stood and began gathering her papers and shoving them into folders. "You know what, never mind. You don't have to change your plans for me. I'll just leave. No big deal."

Damn, somehow he had rattled her, possibly even made her angry. How the hell had that happened with such an innocent conversation? This was precisely why he preferred fleeting moments to long-term affairs; the female mind was a mystery to him. "Have I upset you Miss Sinclair? If it's that important to you to stay and finish your work then I would be more than willing to order in." *I'm just going to have to restrain myself and keep my hands off of you*, he silently advised himself.

She paused for a second and thought about what her attempted exit must look like to him. What in the world had gotten into her? Snapping at her boss was something she had never done before. Being tired had made her lose her damn mind! "Mr. Bainbridge, I'm sorry. I don't know what just got into me, all I can think of is hunger might be making me short tempered." *Or arousal was making me edgy*, she thought. "Please accept my apology and please call me Ember."

"Only if you call me Cole."

"Cole it is," she said with a smile.

"So it's settled then? You'll stay and finish your work? And it's not keeping you from any holiday celebrations?" he asked, hoping the mention of holiday celebrations might make her rethink missing whatever celebration her friend mentioned on the phone.

"I did have a previous engagement, but I need to finish up the research for this sketch and I'll be spending the rest of the weekend with the same people, so I'm fine with making the sacrifice." *Well, that settles that*, he thought.

"What kind of food do you like? All the old reliables deliver to this area: pizza, Chinese, subs, and sushi." Cole said while trying to disengage his gaze from her beautiful smile.

"Well, now it's almost 8:00, and downtown is already crowded, so I think pizza from the place on the corner might be our best bet at this point. In a little while the streets are going to be filled with people. If we order pizza, the delivery guy can just walk it down the block."

"Pizza sounds fine. I'm a cheese, cheese, and more cheese kind of guy. You?"

"I like my cheese with a little bread and sauce, too." She said with a light chuckle that he felt heavily in is groin. "What about wings? I could go for a few wings and bleu cheese dressing. And a Coke." She was getting hungry just thinking about it.

"Pizza, wings, and a Coke. It'll be a holiday feast," he said with a deep laugh that touched her in all the places she wanted him to touch her. "I'll go order it and we can meet up in the lounge to eat. Maybe we can toss some ideas around while we dine. I'll buzz you on the phone when it gets here." And with that he strode out her office, once again reminding her of a jungle cat, and she appreciatively watched him walk away.

* * *

Cole hung up from ordering the pizza and leaned back in his chair. This was not quite going the way he thought. He assumed that it would be easy to get Ember to leave for the night. He had been wrong and now, not only was Ember not leaving, but now they were having dinner together. It was one thing to remain on his best behavior during the day when there were people constantly around them. It was quite another to be alone, at night, eating dinner together. Since Cole was a firm believer in fate and karma, he wondered if his close contact with Ember so soon after finding out that she had a thing for him was a sign that he should try to pursue her. Or maybe he was just fishing for a reason to abandon his original plan to stay away from her. Either way, he was pretty sure that the rest of the night was going to test his restraint. He was a man who was used to going after what he wanted. In the business world he was silent but deadly and rarely showed his hand. Very few people knew just how much he was worth and he liked it that way. It helped that he didn't come from a well to do family and that he remained active in the daily operations of his business. He wasn't some big shot looking down from his place at the top of the company, and that strategy had worked very well for him.

His mother and father had been married for nearly 40 years. He and his two younger brothers and younger sister had been raised middle class, well maybe lower middle class. They never needed for anything, but they certainly weren't rich. What they lacked in abundance of money, they made up for in love and he had fond memories of his childhood. He was very close to his siblings and his parents, and talked to at least one of them daily.

Although Cole never wanted for anything growing up, there were times that he remembered his parents stressing over an unexpected bill or the car breaking down or his sister needing braces. They always made it work, and for that he was grateful, but seeing them stress made him want to never experience that and he wanted to make sure that his parents were able to retire comfortably and enjoy their later years. He knew he also wanted to help his siblings get to where they wanted to be in life. He'd pushed himself through high school, went to college on a scholarship, and worked his way through grad school. He was one of the youngest graduate students in his department.

While in undergrad, at first he studied finance, because he was so focused on having a good financial future. Although he did well in his classes, he didn't have a passion for it. It was in one of his electives, business marketing, that he fell in love with marketing and advertising. He immediately changed his major and the rest, as they say, was history. The finance classes that he took earlier in his education equipped him to make sound financial decisions and, with the help of his cousin Antonio, he made some lucrative investments and business partnerships.

15 years later and his company now had several multimillion-dollar clients while still maintaining smaller mom and pop businesses. It was this down to earth balance that attracted many of his clients; he didn't discriminate and he was hands on with all of his clients. Although he didn't handle every client personally, they all knew his face, were encouraged to contact him if they felt the need to, and he often sat in on client meetings. Soul Escapes Cruiselines was the company's first client in the travel industry, and he wanted to be directly involved with it, so he took the lead on the account. It had been a definite bonus when the head of Soul Escapes had selected Ember to be second in charge. Out of all the senior account managers, the owners felt they connected best with her. Of course this was before Cole had known that she had a thing for him. He had just been content to have a reason to work closely with her.

The intercom buzzed, signaling that the deliveryman was

there with their food. Cole looked at the clock and realized his mind had wandered for nearly an hour. That wasn't usual for him. Typically he was constantly on the go and didn't have time to sit and think. As he rose to go get the food, he thought that he might need to do it more often; it was quite relaxing.

Chapter Three

Her stockings were slowly but surely slipping down her legs and it was getting annoying. Most of the time Ember enjoyed wearing thigh high nylons, they made her feel sexy despite her business clothes, but right now they were slowly driving her insane. Better to just take them off, she decided. With Cole downstairs with the deliveryman, a false sense of solitude led Ember to leave her door open. Kicking off her shoes and hiking her skirt up, she placed her left foot on one of the client chairs in front of her desk, slid her stocking off, and tossed it on her desk.

Following suit with the right leg, she was in the middle of sliding her stocking down when she heard what she thought was a low grunt. Turning her head toward her office door she saw Cole standing there, pizza in one hand and bag of wings in the other, looking like he was about to internally combust. Embarrassed, she snatched her leg down off the chair, retreated around her desk, sat down, and kicked the offending stocking the rest of the way down and off. In a voice that had a slight tremble to it she said, "Food, um, smells good. Pizza always hits the spot."

Hit the spot, huh? he thought. *That's exactly what I want to do.* Instead he said, "Yes, it does. I figured I'd pick you up on the way over to the conference room. You, ahem, have everything settled over there?"

She was hoping he was going to choose to ignore the state he had caught her in. No such luck. "Uh, yes, I am ready. Here let me help you with those bags." Getting up, she realized she was still barefoot and moved to go put her shoes on.

"Leave them off."

Startled by the softly spoken command, Ember froze and locked eyes with Cole. There was that look again, and this time she was positive she wasn't imagining it.

Dammit, he didn't mean to make the request out loud. Now he had to play cleanup. "I'm sure you're more comfortable without them, right? I don't know how women wear high heels all day."

"Yes, I suppose I am."

"Good, then feel free to leave them off. We are the only ones here and your feet don't offend me," he said jokingly, needing to lighten this conversation up a bit.

Wordlessly they walked down the hall together toward the conference room. Without her shoes on, Cole towered over her by more than half a foot. She felt dainty and feminine next to him as he walked next to her in his jungle cat stride. A slight tingle of sexual awareness crawled up the back of her legs and circled her thighs and her breath became a bit labored. *Fight the feeling* she told herself as she double stepped to keep up with him. She held her breath as they walked in the room, hoping to steady her breathing.

"I forgot a file I wanted to show you in my office. Help yourself while I run back to get it," Cole said as he turned and strode back out the door.

Glad to be able to breathe again, Ember began to unpack the food Cole had left on the table. They had worked closely together before, but something seemed different this time.

Maybe it was eating together that was throwing her off a bit. Of course they had working lunches before and the occasional working dinner, but never alone. Realizing the restaurant had forgotten to include napkins with the meal, she reached up into one of the overhead cabinets and pulled down napkins from the stash that was kept there for working lunches and dinner meetings. As she turned around to walk back to the table, the napkins slipped from her hands and fluttered all over the floor.

She got down into a semi squat to pick them all up, wondering where this bit of clumsiness had come from. She was usually at least semi graceful. Her only excuse was that being in such close confines with Cole was wreaking havoc on her ability to function properly. Maybe she should have gone home when he offered to let her go earlier. She had a sinking feeling that she was getting herself into something. As she stood back up she felt a presence behind her and turned to find Cole standing a few feet away. He had obviously been staring at her backside while she was bent over. Her breath caught in her throat as she swung her gaze up and locked eyes with him.

"Did you find the file you were looking for?" she asked in an unsteady voice.

"I did. It was right where I left it. I'll show it to you in a bit. Let's eat," he said while putting the file down on the table. As they sat at the table opposite of each other, Cole thought that this impromptu dinner was really stretching his restraint. Trying to swing his mind back into work mode, he started discussing Soul Escapes. "I know I've said this before, but this account will be big for Commercial Innovations if we land it. We've had some big clients, but Soul Escapes is different. It will open up a whole different sector of advertisement for us. We've never worked in travel before. There's a whole world of opportunities out there once we break in. We land this and it could mean big things for you with this company. You've been here for, what? Four years?" he asked and then bit into a wing.

Who knew that chewing could be sexy? Tearing her eyes

away from his mouth, she took a bite of her pizza to give her time to get her thoughts together. "Yes. Well, it's going on five years now. I started the week after I graduated from college."

Cole remembered how he reacted the first time he had seen her. He had deemed her too young for his taste, but that didn't stop him from looking. She was sexy in a fresh out of college, coed kind of way. At that point she hadn't quite figured out exactly who she wanted to be but he could tell she was getting there and she was very self-assured. Although they never worked directly together, he had seen her in passing over the years and had taken notice of the way she flourished, both physically and within the company. Now, she had grown into her womanhood and damn it looked good on her.

"I'll tell you a little secret if you promise to keep it to yourself," he said in a conspiratorial tone.

"Of course," Ember said.

"I know the owners of Soul Escapes Cruiselines. That doesn't make us a shoe in for the account by any stretch of the mind, but I do know them and that's how I found out they were looking for a new firm to represent them," he said and then wiped his face with his napkin.

"Sometimes you have to go with who you know to show what you know. At least, that's what my father always said. If you don't mind me asking, how do you know them?"

"When I was in college I joined a frat. One of my frat brothers co-owns Soul Escapes; he actually brought me into the frat. You met him when they were here to hear the initial pitches. He was the tall one named Warren. Warren Drake. If I've been in the frat for 14 years, he has to be coming up on 15 years. He's no nonsense though, so he made me go through the same pitching process any other company would go through. He and his business partner Joseph settled on us and an outside agency not connected to the frat that Warren's partner chose.

Knowing his low tolerance for anything less than perfection, I'm honored that he even put me in the running. He can be a hard ass."

"He certainly didn't go easy on any of us when we were doing our pitches. I felt like I was defending my life with all the questions he asked. I bet deep down he's a nice guy," Ember said, wiping her mouth and drinking the last of the water from the bottle she had brought with her from her office.

"No, deep down he's a hard ass," Cole said with a chuckle. "I'm glad he chose you to be the senior exec on this account. If anyone can handle him, it's you. I know it's not easy being a woman in this industry. You can handle him." And just like that, Cole's mind went from talking about Warren to remembering that Ember was indeed a woman, and a fine one at that.

Feeling Cole's gaze change and needing to get out of his line of fire, Ember stood and started clearing the debris from their dinner. "I never joined a sorority but some of my friends did and I know that Greek organizations can be great networking tools. We can lay everything out on the table just as soon as I clear it and we can get back to work."

"Here, let me help you," Cole said and stood just as Ember was reaching over him to grab his plate. Their bodies collided and instant awareness shot through both of them. Cole's pupils dilated with desire and his eyes darkened to nearly black. Ember's entire body began to tingle and that brief contact nearly saturated her panties. Knowing she was in trouble, she backed up to the counter behind her and said, "I, uh, think maybe we should pick this up after the holiday. I think our dinner gave me a touch of the itis and I'm feeling tired."

Knowing he should keep it professional and allow her to take the out she had thrown them both, he opened his mouth to say okay and then shut it before any words came out. His body was awake and seemed to have no intention of simmering down. He knew he had to let her leave but he couldn't bring himself to tell her to go. It was too close, they were too close, even after she backed up, and he still felt her pressed against him. He knew he had to tell her to leave but he couldn't let her go.

Ember watched in amazement as a war ensued on his face. She wasn't sure whether he won or lost but, after a few seconds, he closed the gap between them and looked directly in her eyes.

"I want to taste you," he said as he leaned his body into hers and captured her mouth.

Ember had never tasted chocolate like this. It was thick and full-flavored; the kind of chocolate that you know is too rich for you but you just can't leave it alone. His mouth had to be made of pure cocoa bean. Just the taste of him had saturated her panties and caused her world to become enveloped in an erotic haze. She began to lose her footing so entranced was she by this kiss. Sensing her instability, Cole pulled his mouth from hers long enough to lift her slightly and sit her on the edge of the counter. She scooted back as she spread her legs just wide enough to allow him to fit tightly between them. He leaned forward and captured her mouth again and slid his hands up and down her thighs, lightly caressing her, each time going higher. His tongue danced with hers as he played with the edge of her panties, just as she had done earlier while fantasizing about an encounter just like this.

He kissed his way down her neck and planted kisses on her collarbone while his hand passed the border of her panties and stroked the lips of her sex, which were already slick and wet. He slid his finger in between the folds and dampened it with her wetness, then began to lightly caress her clit. Instantly Ember began to see stars and feel the pressure building behind her walls. She moaned and it was music to Cole's ears. He leaned in and captured her mouth once again and readjusted his hand, so that his pointer and middle fingers slid inside of her, while his thumb created a circular cadence on her clit. She had to break the kiss because she couldn't concentrate on kissing when he was performing sexual sorcery on her. She leaned her forehead against his; their mouths were so close he could feel the puffs of air escape her mouth as she began to grind back on his hand. She rode his hand for what felt like both an eternity and no time at all and then she threw her head back and softly screamed as her body pulsated against his fingers. For a few precious seconds they were suspended on some plane between reality and fantasy. Then they locked eyes.

It was like a bucket of cold water had been tossed on Ember and she jumped back, causing Cole to lose his footing and tumble backwards to the floor and causing her to slide from the counter onto wobbly legs. Breathing heavily, she leaned her weight back on the edge of the counter and locked eyes with Cole again. Instantly she knew she had to get out of there. She stepped over Cole, who was still seated on the floor looking like a deer caught in headlights, dashed down the hallway to grab her shoes and purse, and beelined for the elevator. Luck was on her side and the elevator opened a millisecond after she pushed the button; it was probably still there from when Cole went down to get their food. As she stepped onto the elevator she saw a shadow step into the hall, and she jammed her finger on the button to close the doors then pushed the lobby button. She wasn't interested in talking and she couldn't trust herself not to finish what they had started. She had to get out now.

Cole watched the elevator doors close. The little taste that he had gotten had not been nearly enough and he knew at once that it would not be the last time he was intimate Ember, not with the way she had responded to him. It was just a matter of time.

Chapter Four

Ember was still reeling from her loss of self-control. Her hands clenched the steering wheel tightly as she drove home. She had never allowed a man who wasn't *her man* to touch her the way Cole had. Hell, if she was being completely honest with herself even the few men that she had briefly called *her man* hadn't touched her quite like that. The man had to be some kind of sexual magician. From now on she had to be sure to steer clear of his spells. But how? HOW? How was she supposed to go back to work and act as if that didn't just happen? Like she hadn't felt him touch her most intimate place? Like she hadn't felt the strongest orgasm of her life building up from the moment his lips touched hers? Like she hadn't come apart at his touch?

She was too close to where she needed to be to just leave the company, even though that was the first thought that came to her mind. It would look funny if she just up and left one of the top firms in the area in the middle of vying for a multi-million dollar contract. She doubted that Cole was the type to kiss and tell, but advertising was already a male-dominated field and the last thing she needed to seem was flighty or unstable. When she went back to work on Tuesday she vowed to be all business. She would make it clear to Cole that tonight had been a severe lapse in judgment and it could never happen again. They would finish the proposal, land the account, and then she would stay as far away from him as possible until she decided the time was right to move on and start her own company; hopefully they wouldn't lead another account together again and Soul Escapes would be their only direct contact. That would be her sole focus.

Sighing, she realized she was kidding herself...how the hell was she going to keep her focus after tonight?! She needed to talk this out and she knew just where to go. Taking her right hand off the steering wheel for a split second, Ember pressed the small button on her Bluetooth and said, "Call Cheyenne."

After the third ring she heard a groggy "Ummhello?"

"Chey, it's me. I'm on my way over, so wake up. We need to talk."

"What?! No, no talky. Only sleepy. We can talk when the sun comes up."

"Yes talky! I'm in a situation and it's partially your fault so you have to help me come up with a solution. I'll be there in five minutes. Get up. I'm serious."

"Situation? What situation? And how is it my fault? I haven't seen you in days!"

"True, but you had to go and open your big mouth about sleeping with Cole. Now I'm up shits creek and you *will* be my paddle. Get up! I'm two minutes away."

Awake now, Cheyenne squealed, "Oh my God! You did it! You slept with him?!"

"No!"

"Then why the hell are you waking me up? You're upset because you *didn't* sleep with him?"

"Yes! No! I don't know! I just pulled into your driveway. Get up, I don't want to wait outside and be a feast for these raggedy North Carolina mosquitos."

"You have a key so you can let yourself in Miss Cranky-pants. I'll be downstairs in a minute." And with that Ember heard two beeps that indicated that the call had been ended by Cheyenne.

Leave it to Cheyenne to make light of the situation by calling names. As Ember walked to Cheyenne's front door she steeled herself for a fight. Not only was Cheyenne going to be angry that Ember had awakened her, she was also going to find Ember's reasons for being upset silly. Ember loved her best friend, but Cheyenne had a knack for being very blunt, sometimes at the expense of other's feelings. It wasn't that she tried to purposely hurt people; Cheyenne just had very little patience for what she considered to be nonsense.

Ember let herself into the house and went into the kitchen to start the coffee maker. She hoped that a little caffeine would soothe her nerves. Just as the coffee began to drip into the glass pot, Cheyenne came ambling down the stairs and into the kitchen. *Oh boy*, Ember thought, *she looks exhausted which means I'm about to catch it.* Cheyenne's black hair bonnet was tilted to the right side, making it resemble a beret and a few strands of her jet black hair had escaped confinement. The white remnants of the Noxzema that she religiously slept in were scattered all over her face. Her cinnamon-colored eyes were red and there were sleep creases from her pillow lining the left side of her light brown face. Oddly enough, her blue and yellow silk nightgown wasn't sleep wrinkled at all, which meant that Cheyenne had probably been sleeping in the nude.

"So what is the big problem Ember?" Cheyenne asked as she plopped down into the chair directly across the kitchen table from Ember.

"Why are your eyes so red? Have you been crying or something?" Ember said, momentarily forgetting her plight. Cheyenne rarely cried and Ember was concerned.

"Now why would I be crying? You woke me up, that's all. Let's solve your crisis so I can go back to slumber land."

"Cole kissed me!" Ember blurted out.

"And?" Cheyenne said as if she was waiting for Ember to actually state the problem.

"He kissed me and. . . uh . . . put his hand in places! And I let him kiss me! I think I may have even encouraged it! This is all your fault, with all your talk about Cole and sexing on the job---"

Ember was silenced by the near hysterical laughter coming from Cheyenne. "Just what the hell is so funny?!" she asked, looking at Cheyenne like she had lost all of her faculties.

"*You* are funny!" Cheyenne replied while gasping for breath. "You're sitting at my kitchen table in the middle of the night losing your mind about this man fingering you? And I think you're really mad because you liked it. That is one of the funniest things I have ever heard. Are we twelve again? Is this your first kiss? Did you get felt up behind the bleachers?"

"First of all, your fast ass had your first kiss at twelve; I waited until I was a respectable fourteen. Second, it's not just a kiss. And it was a kiss with my boss! I've worked hard to achieve all that I have and I truly like my job. If things become awkward because of this kiss, it will be me who has to leave the company. Cole can't leave; he owns the place. What am I going to do?"

"Kiss him again. Maybe this time you could return the favor and--"

"Cheyenne Jade! That is not an option!"

"Why not?! You know he wants you; he made that abundantly clear tonight. Why wouldn't you enjoy it? Just make sure that the two of you set ground rules. That way if or when it ends you both will know where you stand. It's that simple," Cheyenne said, slapping her hand on the table. She was growing tired of this conversation and wanted to get back to bed.

"What ground rules? Wait, don't answer that. It makes no

never mind, there will be no affair between Cole and I. There's too much at stake. Plus you know I would never have an office romance, and certainly not with my boss."

"Why not? Bosses are men too, well male bosses anyway. And often they are very sexy men, as is the case with your boss," Cheyenne said, licking her lips.

"I would never begin anything sexual with Cole. Violet taught me that romance with a boss is a very bad idea." As soon as the words were out of her mouth, Ember regretted them. Not only because they opened the not quite healed wound caused by the disappearance of her close friend, but also because of the wave of anger that washed over Cheyenne's face with every word she spoke.

"I can't believe you!" Cheyenne ground out. "I have entertained your ridiculous over analyzation of this situation thus far because I know you and how anal you can be, but now you have really lost your damn mind. How many times do I have to tell you that you can't use Violet's extreme situation as a crutch? You can't---"

"I'm not! It just made me aware of---"

"No, it gave you something else to hide behind! You hide behind "situations" that have "taught" you lessons. Before Violet died---"

"We don't know if Violet is dead!" Ember declared in a near scream.

Cheyenne stared Ember straight in the eyes, visually daring her to further argue that point. "Before. Violet. Died. It was Shannon, remember? Shannon gave up her dream of being a real estate agent to marry Jason and for a while she was happy being a stay at home wife. Then Jason left her. After that you said you weren't going to pursue a relationship because you didn't want to risk all that you have worked for."

"It's not the sa---"

"Yes it is. When we were teenagers you used your parents screwed up marriage as an excuse to not get close to guys. You said you didn't want to get pregnant, be forced to get married, and have your husband resent you. It's a wonder you even lost your virginity in high school."

"Why am I being faulted for being cautious and trying not to repeat the mistakes of everyone around me?"

"You're not being cautious; you're being scared. I know you think that I'm too blunt at times but I refuse to spare your feelings when all you're doing is hurting yourself. Everyone needs a companion, everyone needs love, hell everyone needs the release that good sex can bring. Why are you denying yourself?'

"Not everyone is focused on sex! I am different from you; I don't need sexual release to be able to function in everyday life!" Even as she said it, Ember knew that was a lie, not three hours ago she had attempted one of her ménage a mois to get her mind back on track.

"Ember, I think you are under the misthought that you are functioning. You aren't, you just exist. You go to work. You come home. You miss family events to work. You miss girl's night out to work. You even miss church to work. What kind of life is that? Where is your fun? Where is the light?"

"This coming from a woman who is nothing but "light"? You see who you want, when you want, with no regard for time or propriety. You run off and take pictures when you want; you have no structure in your life. You spent all that time in school to be a physical therapist and won't get a job in your field. If it wasn't for the fact that you made a living from your photography, you'd be destitute. You don't have the discipline to function in the real corporate world!" Ember felt bad as soon as she said it, but her anger prevented her from stopping. She was, after all, having the core of her life attacked.

"That's right! I couldn't function in your world and I have no desire to do so! I do what and who I want, where and when

I want. It makes me happy to be this way. If that makes me a flaky whore, then so be it. At least I'm living!" Taking a deep breath to steady herself she said: "You know what? I can't deal with this at dark-thirty in the morning. I'm going upstairs and back to bed. You know how to let yourself out."

Slowly getting up from her chair, Cheyenne leveled a hard gaze at Ember and said her last piece. "If you keep living your life this way you may as well be as dead as Violet."

Chapter Five

Ember was wet and ready from him. He could tell as he ran his fingers up and down her thighs and leaned in between them. Her beautiful naked body shivered and Cole was sure it was from his touch rather than from being cold. She looked like a woman on fire and it had him ready to combust. Knowing he was testing his own patience, he decided he needed a taste before he slid inside of her. Connecting his gaze with hers, he slowly moved down her body, planting random kisses as he descended. Once he was in the right position, he placed both of her legs over his shoulders. Ember gripped the sheets in a haze of erotic expectation as he lowered his head.

The moment his tongue touched her clit she bucked her hips and released a cry of ecstasy. He immediately knew that she was his new favorite flavor; her taste was indescribable and he couldn't get enough. He devoured her, literally diving in face first and she arched her hips to give him unrestricted access to pleasure her. Before long her legs began to tighten around his shoulders and he knew she was close to cumming. He focused all of his attention on her bud of pleasure and was rewarded with her scream of fulfillment as she pulsated against his mouth and bucked her hips. Damn, she tasted sweet.

The next thing Cole knew, the sound of Crossover by EPMD was ringing in his ears. He sat up straight, realizing he was on the couch in his office and, unfortunately, not between Ember's legs. *What a hell of a dream*, he thought as he leaned down on the floor to grab his phone, whose ringtone was what had awakened him. Seeing his brother's name scrolling across the phone screen, he picked up, bracing himself to hear some static.

"Good morning Rock."

"Good morning hell. I'm going to assume that you're going to be late since you were supposed to be here yesterday. I'm going to also assume that you know I've been catching the heat for your inability to arrive anywhere on time," Rock said, annoyance dripping from his voice.

"Yes, I am still in Raleigh but I will be getting on the road shortly. I had to stay late last night to work on some things," Cole said.

"What was so urgent that you couldn't leave and drive to Charlotte yesterday like you promised mom?"

"I . . . listen, who's the older brother here? Be easy or you'll catch a jab to the throat when I get there."

"Yeah right, what's her name?"

"Look, I know I said I was going to be there yesterday evening but we're working on this big proposal for Warren's cruise line and because it's so big I'm directly involved in creating the pitch and—"

"Seriously, who are you talking to right now? I know all about Soul Escapes and how big it is. That doesn't answer my question. What's her name?"

"I don't know what you're talking about –"

"You clearly have forgotten which one of us has the higher IQ. If this was strictly work related you would be going on and on about this pitch and that angle and blah blah blah. Instead, you're all clammed up and trying to pull that I'm older crap.

There's a woman involved. The least you can do is tell me since mom is convinced I should have picked you up on the way into town even though that would have been waaaaaaaay out of my way," Rock said, his annoyance clear.

"First, the only place you're smarter than me is in that twisted head of yours. Second, it's complicated and I need to get up and get on the road so I don't have time to tell you right now. I'm stuck with you for the next three days. We'll talk when I get there."

"I knew there was a woman. I'll give you until you get here but then you come up off the information. And I would get a move on; Onyx just got here and she had to fly down from New York. If Micah beats you home all the way from California, there will be hell to pay."

"Dammit. Okay. I'm gone. See you later," Cole said as he hit the off button on the screen, jumped up, and grabbed his keys and wallet off his desk. He lived the closest to his parents and if he was the last one to get to Charlotte, there would indeed be hell to pay. He quickly strode to the elevator, punched the down button, and remembered watching the doors close on Ember as she left the night before. He wanted to call her, but he didn't want to disturb her holiday and he wasn't 100% sure she would even talk to him right now. The way she flew out of there last night was a clear indication that, while her body had been more than willing, mentally she had not anticipated what happened between them. It was probably better to give her a couple of days to process everything and enjoy the holiday. He fully intended to pursue her but it could wait until after Memorial Day. Plus, he wanted to talk to Rock and Micah and get their take on the situation. Although he was the oldest, he didn't mind getting advice from his bothers every once in a while.

* * *

When Ember woke up the next morning, before she opened her eyes, she prayed that some kind of miracle happened and she got to redo the day before. She reached over and grabbed her cell phone. No such luck; it was Saturday. For a moment she considered pulling the covers back over her head and refusing to face the world. Though it was tempting, she only had a few days to figure this all out and she needed all the time she could get. Sighing heavily, she rolled out of bed and drug herself in the bathroom to splash some water on her face. When she looked in the mirror she realized that no amount of water splashing was going to help and she reached over to turn the shower on. She had hardly slept last night as she juggled being mad at Cheyenne and stressed about what happened with Cole. Ember wasn't worried about any lasting effects from the fight with Cheyenne. They'd had much worse fights and she had to admit that some of the things Cheyenne said were true. They would be fine by the end of the cookout tonight. *Cole is a completely different story*, she thought as she stepped into the shower.

The hot water hit her and she instantly started to feel better. As her mind began to clear, she started problem solving. She had to find a way to get things back to strictly business so that she could finish her plan. When she graduated from college she had a plan. Step one of that plan was to land a position with Commercial Innovations. Cole was one of the few men of color who owned and operated an extremely successful advertising firm. There were no women of color then or now that had accomplished such a feat. Ember wanted to be the first. Advertising was a male dominated field for a very long time and it was specifically white male dominated until Cole stepped on the scene. Ember wanted to be the female version of Cole, only bigger and better.

During her junior year, when it had been time to search for an internship for her senior year, she thanked her lucky stars that her HBCU was located in Durham, less than a half hour from Commercial Innovations' downtown Raleigh location. She had been thrilled when she landed one of three intern spots at Commercial Innovations and naively thought that she would study right under the advertising genius that was Cole Bainbridge. Instead, she had been stuck with an entry-level ad man who was only a few years older than her and not very good at his job. By the time the internship had ended, he was no longer employed there and she had been moved to work under a department manager. The move had proved beneficial for her, though, because that manager recommended her for an entry-level position that came open the week before her internship ended and by the time she graduated she had been hired. She planned to stay for 5-7 years, work her way up the ranks, make a name for herself, and then open her own firm by her 30th birthday. She had been on track until she veered into that train wreck last night.

She stepped out of the shower, grabbed her towel to dry off, and then slipped into her favorite fluffy robe. She was no closer to a solution now than when she had stepped into the shower but at least she physically felt better. Mentally, not so much. She went downstairs, turned on her coffee maker, and sat down at her kitchen table to look out of the window. Just like at work, at home she looked out of windows when her mind drifted.

Shit. Shit, shit, shit, shit. She had to find a way around this. She was seriously considering hiding out in the house and skipping the cookout when her phone rang. She saw Gabriella's name flashing across the screen and hit the speaker button.

"Hey girl."

"Feliz día conmemorativo!" Gabriella was the perfect combination of feisty Latina and down black chick. Hearing her voice made Ember smile for the first time in at least 12 hours.

"Happy Memorial Day to you too girlie. What time should I be at your house?"

"Anytime you want to girl. You know mi casa es su casa. But before you come, you and Cheyenne need to squash whatever happened to make her so bitchy when I called her this morning. I asked her what her problem was and she said it was you and then said she had to go. What happened between me leaving her house at like nine last night and this morning?"

Ember sighed. Apparently Cheyenne wasn't ready to let bygones be bygones just yet. "We got into it last night. I almost had sex with Cole Bainbridge and—"

"Wait what?! What did you just say? Nope, uh uh, you don't just get to say something like that and not explain. I changed my mind. You get over here right now. Now girl now."

"But I was about to have breakfast and I need some coffee. I just got out the shower and –"

"Good, so your culo is already clean. Get on some clothes and get over here. I have breakfast and coffee. See you in 20. Don't forget your pies and cake. I already know that's what you made for the cookout!" Gabriella said and quickly hung up.

Ember sighed and stood up to go get dressed. There was no arguing with Gabriella and she wasn't in the mood to try. Where Ember and Cheyenne were often two extremes, Gabriella was right in the middle. Maybe she could help her come up with a plan of action for this mess she had gotten herself into.

Chapter Six

An hour later, on the way over to Gabriella's house, Ember decided that, although she fully intended to give Cheyenne the side eye for at least an hour into the cookout, she was actually looking forward to spending time with Cheyenne and Gabriella. Ember and Cheyenne had grown up together; both were only children and became the sisters that they had wished for as very young children.

Growing up in south Florida wasn't easy. Ember had been raised by a single parent with no close family and Cheyenne had grown up just above the poverty line, but they went through it together and always had each other's back. Neither wanted to spend any more time in Florida than necessary, so they both applied to out of state colleges with the knowledge that they would attend the same school. When Cheyenne got a full ride scholarship to North Carolina Central University, Ember made that her school of choice as well and landed a scholarship of her own.

Freshman year Ember and Cheyenne were broke but still wanted to be fly so they decided to go to the local cosmetology school to get their hair done. The second time they went, they met Gabriella who is in school to be a stylist. The semester after she graduated from cosmetology school, Gabriella joined them at the university to pursue a degree in business. Sophomore year Cheyenne met a girl named Violet in a class they were taking together. The four of them had become inseparable.

Ember pulled up in front of Gabriella's townhouse and parked in the driveway. As she got out the car she adjusted her pink sundress and then walked towards the front door, pulling out the spare key she had. When she pulled the screen door open, she saw that the inner door was slightly open, which was Gabriella language for don't bother knocking just come in. Ember pushed the door open and called out to Gabriella.

"How many times do I have to warn you about the dangers of leaving your damn front door open?"

Gabriella called from the living room, "One, nobody but you and me knew it was open until your big mouth just blasted it across the neighborhood and two I wish a *singao* would. I'd put a bullet clear between their eyes before they got in the house good." Since Gabriella had been raised by her black mother, she didn't speak Spanish well, but she was quite fluent in Spanish curse words.

"Uh huh, you're real tough until someone runs up in here," Ember said as she set the pies and cake on the kitchen counter, joined Gabriella in the living room and plopped down on the couch next to her. Gabriella was wearing a blood red maxi dress and the color looked amazing on her.

"Whatever. Now spill about the almost sex and explain to me how this involves Cheyenne because I'm not understanding that part at all," Gabriella said.

After Ember relayed the whole story, Gabriella leaned back and said, "Well that's a damn mess."

"Thanks, that's exactly what I needed to hear."

"It's the truth, but the good news is that the situation with Cheyenne is an easy fix. Just tell her she made some valid points and you're sorry you upset her."

"I'm sorry?! She came at me crazy and I'm sorry? Nope. It's not even going down like that. Uh uh."

"You woke her up in the middle of the night, you didn't want to hear her advice after you woke her up *for advice* and you basically called her a slack ass. You need to say sorry babe."

"Well shit, she called me a prude and told me I was dead like Violet, who isn't dead!"

"So she needs to apologize too then, but you know she's not going to go first. And you two fools are not going to ruin my cookout because you want to fight over nonsense. And with Violet, you know Cheyenne thinks that Violet killed herself and we just haven't found her body yet. She's thought that from the beginning and I don't think anything you say or do is going to change her mind. It doesn't help that they lived together and she passes Violet's room every day. It doesn't matter that she boxed her things up. The room and the space they shared are still there. You know Cheyenne is cut and dry, black and white. Violet never just up and disappeared before. To Cheyenne that can only mean she's dead. Honestly, I'm not even sure what to believe anymore. It's been almost a year and not a trace of her. Nothing. I just don't know anymore."

"No. Violet would never kill herself. Never," Ember argued. "Don't let Cheyenne convince you otherwise. Violet's out there and there's some kind of explanation for this. I know there is."

"I know you believe that, I just don't know what I believe anymore and if months of private detectives produced nothing, we are not going to figure it out today. What we do need to figure out is how you are going to deal with your hot-for-boss situation."

"You're right," Ember sighed. "What am I going to do? All this hard work and sticking to my plan and I go and blow it on a few minutes of . . . I can't lie it was a few minutes of ecstasy, but it wasn't worth screwing myself." Ember almost laughed at the irony of the words but the severity of her situation prevented her from indulging.

"Well, since you've made it clear that you won't be indulging in an affair with Cole, I see you having two choices. One, you go back to work and ask for a meeting with him. In the meeting you explicitly state that you don't want anything like that to happen again. If he seems to want to argue you can throw in something about sexual harassment for good measure. Or, two, you can leave and start your own firm now."

"No! I can't go out on my own yet! It's not time!" Ember said in a near panic.

"Why can't you? You have the ability, you have the experience and you damn sure have the funds," Gabriella said raising her perfectly arched eyebrows in question.

Ember fell quiet because she didn't have an answer. Cheyenne and Gabriella were the only two people in the entire state of North Carolina who knew exactly what Ember's background was.

Although their marriage hadn't lasted, Ember's parents had provided well for their daughter. When her parents broke up her mother picked up a pen and began writing everything that came to mind. Five years later she was a best-selling author and she had put out at least two bestsellers a year for the next 13 years. Her sudden death during Ember's junior year of college had devastated her.

Ember's father was already quite wealthy when he and her mother divorced and he continued to work in the family real estate business. When he died just before her 24th birthday, he left her a substantial inheritance that she had placed in the bank to help her build her company when the time was right. Couple that with the money she had received at her mother's death, including being the beneficiary for all royalties her mother acquired after she died, and she was quite well off, though she told no one and lived well below her means. Gabriella was right; she certainly did have the funds.

"But this account we are working on, Soul Escapes Cruiselines, is a huge account. If I can put my name on landing this account and maintaining it with increased sales on their end, I can leave Cole's company having made a serious name for myself in the big leagues. I would be insane to pass that chance up and leave now, right?"

"Then I guess you better put your big girl panties on and go in there first thing Tuesday morning and tell him hands off or else."

Ember let out a big sigh, wishing she could avoid the conflict completely but knowing that was impossible at this point. "Well, I came here looking for a plan of action and that's what I got, right? I do feel better at least knowing how I'm going to handle it. And I have a few days to, as Cheyenne says, get some nuts about myself. I'll be ready to face him on Tuesday," Ember said with a bit more confidence than she felt.

"Okay, so bonus question: If Cole wasn't your boss, would you indulge? From what you said, the little taste you got . . . was . . . gooooood." Gabriella leaned in and whispered the last word.

"I don't have time for romance, sex, or anything like that right now ---"

"And that's your damn problem heffa!" Both Ember and Gabriella nearly jumped off the couch as Cheyenne's loud accusation startled them. They turned to see her stride into the room holding a large tin foil covered plastic bowl containing her famous seafood salad. She was dressed in a teal halter top, cream shorts, and gold sandals. Her turquoise earrings, bracelet, and toe ring completed the outfit.

"Aw shit, I was just getting to the good stuff! I knew I shouldn't have given you a spare key!" Gabriella said, knowing that the conversation was going to shift to Ember and Cheyenne's beef now. In an effort to head off the argument she saw coming, Gabriella announced, "Well, Ember and I came up with a solution to her problem so there's no need to even talk about it now. You should go put that seafood salad in the fridge before it spoils."

"Unless her solution involves her being up under that man, I think the plan sucks. And don't try to distract me with this food, I live ten minutes away; it takes hours for food to spoil. I also brought some rum with me. I figured we would need as much alcohol as we could get in our systems today."

Gabriella busted out laughing and got up to grab the bowl. "Girl, who are you fooling? We both know that alcohol is your way of saying sorry. Give me that bowl and you two hug this shit out." After Gabriella took the food into the kitchen, Cheyenne sat down on the couch next to Ember.

"Look dammit. You need some fun in your life. I'm not saying go out and join an erotic circus or something but all work and no play is a wasted life. And since you are so focused on work, how perfect is it that play is presenting itself in the form of your sexy ass boss? If nothing else, losing Violet taught me that our time on earth is not guaranteed and you need to enjoy every minute of it."

"I still say we haven't lost Violet but that's for another time. On Tuesday morning I'm going to request a meeting with Cole and tell him that it can't happen again and get back to my career plan. I know you worry about me but I'm good. I really am. And once my firm is up and running, I'll be able to take a break and get some of this life you keep telling me to get. You just stay on me and don't let me get too caught up, okay?"

Cheyenne sighed, understanding that Ember was hell bent on doing things her way. "You know I will. I love ya girl." Rising, she declared, "Okay, beef over. Now let's get this party started!"

Chapter Seven

Cole strode into his parent's home four hours after getting on the road and saw all three of his siblings sitting in the den smirking at him. *I knew I should have just gotten on the road and showered here* he thought as he braced himself for whatever his mother was about to throw his way.

He set his overnight bag down in the foyer, sat down next to his youngest brother, Micah, and tried to blend in like he had been there for a while.

"So you're just going to slide in, not say any kind of hello, and think that mom isn't going to notice that you're just getting here?" his sister Onyx said as she rolled her perfectly made up eyes.

"Oh, I heard him come in. And I know he doesn't think that showing up an entire day late is going to go unnoticed," his mother, Isabel said as she walked into the den. Even at nearly 60 years old, she was still a beauty and moved with grace. Her shoulder length gray hair was pinned on the sides, no doubt to keep her tresses out of the way while she cooked. Her eyes matched her hair, a hereditary trait on her mother's side of the family and her 5"6' frame was still trim and fit. "Get yourself up and give me a hug. I bet you're the only son in the world that lives less than four hours away from his parents and only makes it home once in a blue moon."

Cole stood and wrapped his mother in a bear hug and then kissed her on the forehead. "I'm sorry I'm late mom, something came up at the office and I had to delay leaving." Rock coughed in his hand and said bullshit, and Cole shot his brother a deadly look.

"I'm sure it is bullshit son, but no one asked your opinion," Isabel said to her middle son before turning back to her first born. "No problem, you can just stay an extra day to make up for it. Your brothers and sister aren't leaving until the end of next week, the least you can do is give us until Tuesday," she said and then turned to walk back into the kitchen.

"No, I have to get back ---" Cole started to say but stopped short when his mother turned around and cut her eyes at him. That look terrified him as a child and he was not a fan of it as an adult. "I, ahem, guess one extra day won't hurt," he said as he heard his siblings snickering in the background.

"Good," she said, turning her smile back on. "You got here just in time. The food is just coming off the grill and all the sides have been put out. Y'all go wash up. We eat in five minutes," she said and then walked back to the kitchen.

"You know she just played you, right?" Onyx said barely containing a laugh as she stood up with her brothers to go wash up.

"You know I didn't ask you, right?" Cole said and attempted to trip her as she brushed past him. He missed and she turned around and licked her tongue out at him and then quickened her pace to the bathroom.

"Hey you two, thanks for coming to my aid back there. You really had my back," Cole said sarcastically to his brothers.

"Nobody was trying to ride the trouble train with your ass. And dad's out in the backyard smoking a cigar with Uncle Duck so we had no back up either? Yeah, you're on your own," Rock said, shaking his head.

"Yeah, I'm with Rock. But I do want to know about the mystery woman who made you late. She got a sister? Younger or older, doesn't matter," Micah said. He was undeniably the family gigolo. Where Cole was too jaded and too busy for a long-term relationship, Micah had the time but didn't have the want. He preferred his relationships short term and of a sexual nature.

"I see someone has been running his mouth," Cole said turning his gaze to his middle brother. "You're talking about something and don't even know what you're talking about."

"I used my superior deductive skills to figure out what was going on." Rock was a private investigator and if his large clientele was any indication, he was a damn good one.

"Deductive skills my ass. And it was work related . . . she works with me."

"Oh damn, this is gonna be good," Micah said rubbing his hands together.

"Why is everyone out here but you boys?! We want to bless the food!" They heard their mother yell down the hall.

"Poker game tonight. I'll tell you if you promise not to act like assholes," Cole said as they quickened their pace down to the bathroom.

"I never make a promise I can't keep," Rock said.

"Cosign," Micah agreed.

Cole knew he was in for a long night.

* * *

Later that night the three Bainbridge brothers gathered in their parents' den to play poker and discuss Cole's mystery woman. They had been doing this since they were kids; playing poker and talking things out. Cole was the oldest, but he and his brothers were what you called stair step siblings. Cole was

36, Rock was 35, and Micah was 33, almost 34. Not only were they close in age, but they were also nearly identical. All were the same height and nearly the same weight, however Rock had his mother's gray eyes and Micah had curly hair and wore it in a mini afro while his brothers both wore their hair cut low. Their personalities are what clearly set them apart. While Cole was stoic and serious, Rock was cautious and suspicious, which was perfect for a PI. Micah was adventurous and free-spirited and that suited him well for his career as a reality TV writer and producer. They made quite a trio.

As Rock dealt the cards, Cole filled his brothers in on what transpired 24 hours ago. By the time he finished the story and gave background information, they were well into their second hand of poker.

"So you either have one hell of an office romance on your hands or one hell of a sexual harassment suit," Rock said, shaking his head.

"Indeed. What would you do if you were me?"

"I've seen too many of these work relationships go bad for me to have one. I'm just being honest. All kinds of crazy shit happens. She could be deranged, married, a gold digger, anything. I've even seen bodies turn up from a work romance. It seems like it's so much easier to get a woman not affiliated with your job and avoid all the insanity that could happen," Rock explained, dealing the next hand of cards.

"Man, don't listen to Mr. Play It Safe. You said yourself that you heard her friend admit that she's been interested in you for a long time. And she obviously didn't object to messing around at first. She probably just got spooked because you're her boss. If you make it clear that it won't affect her job or her place in the company I think she'll be game," Micah said leaning back in his chair and studying his cards.

"This fool is going to get you sued," Rock said shaking his head. "Women are all over the place. If you want one, go get one you won't have to see every day if things go south. That's just good sense man and you know that the good sense train rode right by Micah and never came back."

"And the last time you got some was when . . . ?" Micah asked laying down a full house.

"Around the last time you minded your damn business," Rock said, laying down a straight flush. "Now give me all your money, baby brother."

Cole threw his cards down. "Yall aren't helping, you know. With each of you on one side, I need a tie breaker or something. Maybe we should ask dad---"

"Or you could ask your only sibling you have that has good sense," Onyx said as she strolled into the room, plopped down on the couch, and pulled out her phone to send a text message.

"We've been telling you for over 20 years that these are guys only games. When are you going to get that through your head, brat?" Cole said, flicking a card at her.

"Around the same time that you figure out I don't care," she said, picking up the card and flicking it back. "If 20 years of me sitting right outside that door listening to all of your conversations hasn't taught you to look before you talk, then I got nothing for ya."

"I think all that hair is clouding your brain and making you too mouthy," Rock said pointing to the large curly afro that Onyx proudly wore.

"Hi, hater," she said to Rock and then turned her attention to Cole. "I think the answer to your problem is simple."

"Oh yeah, and that would be?"

"Ask her what she wants. You three Neanderthals have been sitting here debating whether Cole was going to walk away or pursue this woman but shouldn't he know if she wants him to walk away or pursue? Doesn't she get a say?" Onyx asked with a hint of agitation in her voice.

"Feminism has arrived at the table," Micah joked and Onyx threw a throw pillow at him.

"Ever since you went au natural you ---"

"Don't even finish that sentence, Rock," Onyx said, her gray eyes identical to his flashing a warning. "My choice to take chemicals out of my hair and wear it the way God made it has nothing to do with you three fools thinking like Cro-Magnon man. If you did decide to pursue her but she doesn't want to be pursued, what were you going to do? Club her over the head and say 'You Cole woman now. Unga bunga'? Gimme a break."

"Although she's being her usually bratty self, Onyx does have a point. I'm overthinking how to approach this. I should just ask Ember where she wants to go with this. When I return to work on Tuesday---"

"You mean Wednesday unless you want to risk mom knocking you out," Micah interjected.

"Damn, right. Okay, when I return to work on Wednesday, I'll just ask her to step in my office for a quick meeting and ask her what she wants. That seems simple enough."

"And if she says she doesn't want to pursue anything with you?" Onyx asked.

"Then I'll just have to convince her otherwise. I can be very persuasive," Cole said reaching for the deck of cards, satisfied with his course of action.

"And there's the return of the caveman. I swear you three old dogs can't be taught new tricks," she said as she stood up and pushed the ottoman up to the table.

"Who are you calling old? You're getting up there yourself. I'm sure you have some gray hair hiding in that massive show-piece you have on your head," Micah said.

"Twenty-five is nowhere near you guys in your thirties and don't you forget it. Deal me in. I feel like making some money off of you cavemen tonight."

They dealt her in and she did indeed make money that night.

Chapter Eight

When Ember's alarm went off on Tuesday morning, she pulled the comforter over her head in an attempt to avoid what she knew she had to do that day. The last few days had been so relaxing for her and she didn't look forward to getting back into the grind of work, especially with such a large account looming over her head, although she did look forward to landing the Soul Escapes account and adding it to her portfolio. And of course there was Cole and the conversation she knew she had to have with him. Talking the situation out with Gabriella really helped ease her mind, but now her heart was racing thinking about being alone with Cole again, even if it was to tell him they wouldn't be intimate again.

Ember thought back to Saturday and how she and her friends had such a good time at the cookout. Quite a few people had stopped by throughout the day and well into the night. Several hands of spades and tunk had been played and someone even pulled out a set of dominoes. The music had been the perfect mix of old school and new school and she thoroughly enjoyed herself. She knew that Cheyenne was right and she needed to loosen up a bit but she didn't want to lose focus of her plan. There had to be an in between, right?

Ember's alarm went off for a second time and she knew she had to get up; she didn't want to be late and have to tell her boss to keep his hands to himself in the same day. She got up, walked over to her closet and picked out a black pencil skirt and a dark yellow sleeveless peplum blouse. She pulled out her favorite and most comfortable black pumps and laid her bra, panties, and thigh highs on the bed before walking into the bathroom and turning the shower on. As she stepped in the shower, she once again thought about how relaxing the last few days had been.

She spent Sunday and Monday sleeping late, reading, and catching up on all the TV shows she missed while working late. She truly enjoyed doing nothing and wished she had a few more days to relax. At that moment she decided to take a vacation after they landed the Soul Escapes account. She even thought about possibly booking a cruise with Soul Escapes. She hadn't been exaggerating when she had told Cole that the ships and their amenities were amazing. A nice cruise, away from everything and everybody, was just what she needed. Mind made up, she finished her shower and got ready to head to work, feeling a lot better about going in knowing that a much-needed vacation was on the horizon.

* * *

As she stepped into the elevator at work, Ember thought about the situation with Cole again and wondered if things would be different if she met him under different circumstances. If he wasn't her boss, her stepping stone to greatness, if it wouldn't ruin her plan, would she indulge in an affair with him? Shaking her head, she wiped the thought away. No use in wasting time thinking about what would never be. She walked into her office, noted the blinking light on her phone indicating she had messages waiting to be listened to, and walked back down the hall towards Cole's office. It was best to get this conversation over with as soon as possible; she didn't want it looming over her head while she was trying to work.

"Hi Cecile, is Mr. Bainbridge available for a quick meeting?" Ember asked as she stepped in front of the desk that belonged to the executive administrative assistant.

"Hi Ember! Mr. Bainbridge called a little while ago and said he would be out today. He didn't give a reason. I hope he's all right; he hardly ever takes days off. Do you think something might be wrong with him? How was your holiday?" Cecile said in her usual chattery way. Ember felt like she had swallowed her tongue. Well shit. Of course it was her luck that the man who never takes a day off would take the day off when she needed to talk to him. Because that's life, right? Now she would have to psych herself up again tomorrow to come in here and have this talk with Cole. It was like this situation would never end. She realized her face must be twisted when she saw Cecile looking at her curiously. Ember fixed her face quickly. She was sweet but Cecile was also the office gossip and she didn't need Cecile thinking that she had anything to gossip about concerning her.

"My holiday was great. I spent it with my two best friends and relaxed. How was yours?"

"Oh it was fine," Cecile said dismissively, preferring to stay focused on Ember. "How come you didn't go home to your family? You're from Florida, right? I never hear about you traveling back home . . ." Cecile said, eyeing her like she was the next stop on the gossip train.

"Oh, I hate to fly and it's such a long trip to drive in such a few days. I'll check back in with Mr. Bainbridge tomorrow. See you later!" Ember said as she quickly eased her way out of anymore probing questions. No one knew her background and she intended to keep it that way.

On her way back to her office Ember walked by the conference room and had flashbacks of the time she had spent in there with Cole. Immediately she felt herself grow warm and her lower half go liquid. She knew that her body was about to start doing things she wanted to ignore so she quickened her pace and closed the door behind her when she entered her office.

Deciding she was going to make the best out of this day, even though she would probably be distracted thinking about having to talk to Cole tomorrow, Ember figured she should start with checking her voicemail. She sat down at her desk, grabbed her notepad and pen, picked up the phone and dialed her code. She immediately recognized the voice in the first message.

"Ms. Sinclair, this is Warren Drake. My partner and I have a proposition for you. Please call me back as soon as you can. This is a time sensitive matter. Talk to you soon."

Ember was instantly intrigued. Mr. Drake had been impressed with her initial pitch and she wondered if it had blown away the competition enough that Soul Escapes had decided to go forward with them already. Wouldn't that be wonderful? She decided not to waste anytime calling Warren Drake back. He picked up on the second ring.

"Good morning Mr. Drake, this is Ember Sinclair from Commercial Innovations returning your call."

"Ms. Sinclair, glad to hear back from you so soon. How was your holiday?"

"It was very good, quite relaxing. I hope yours was as well."

"It was indeed. Listen, I'll cut right to the chase because I have a meeting to get to in just a few minutes. Frank and I discussed it and we would like you to join us on our seven day cruise leaving on Thursday. We think that the best way for you to get a feel for our company and what we offer is to experience it firsthand. Of course this would be free of charge and we would give you our best package so that you could experience everything. What do you think?"

"Mr. Drake, that is very generous. Very, very generous. I would have to check with Mr. Bainbridge to make sure he could spare me during that time but I would love to cruise with Soul Escapes."

"Great news. I've already talked to Cole and he said he would have no problem giving you paid time off since you would technically still be working. He also accepted the invitation I extended to him as well."

Ember almost choked on the air she was breathing.

"Wait, so it's Mr. Bainbrindge and myself attending?" Ember asked trying to keep the panic out of her voice. The absolute last thing she needed to do was go on a cruise with Cole.

"Yes, you two are the leads on our proposal, so of course we would want both of you to get the full Soul Escapes experience. We have also invited representatives from the other company we are looking at. We want it to be fair, of course."

"Yes, of course," Ember said, knowing there was absolutely no way she could back out of this. Her not attending could give the other company an advantage over them and that could be disastrous. She was trapped.

"Ms. Sinclair I have to run to this meeting but I'm glad we got everything settled. I'll have my assistant email you the information. The ship is sailing from Charleston, South Carolina. You'll be able to get transportation down there, right?"

"Yes, that won't be a problem."

"Wonderful. I really must go now or I'll be late. See you in a few days. Bye."

"Goodbye Mr. Drake," Ember said, and then laid the phone down in the cradle. She leaned back in her chair and exhaled, not realizing she had been holding her breath. What in the actual hell had just happened? Did she just agree to go on a seven day cruise with Cole Bainbridge? She looked at the clock and saw that it wasn't even 10am yet. She needed to get out of there but it was too early to even take an early lunch. She was stuck even though, with this new debacle, there wasn't a chance in hell she was going to be productive. She picked up her cell phone and called Gabriella.

"Hey girl, what's up?" Gabriella said after the third ring.

"Hey, are you with a client?" Ember asked, again trying to keep the panic out of her voice.

"No. I'm actually not booked at all today. You know the week after a big holiday is always dead, so I scheduled all of my regular clients for the weekend so I could have a few back-to-back days off. I'll pick back up Saturday. You sound weird. What's wrong? Did you have the talk with your boss? How did it go?"

"I don't even know where to begin. Can you meet me for lunch at 12? Cheyenne doesn't have another assignment until the beginning of June, so can you get her and meet me at Beasley's?"

"Is it that bad? Are you okay?"

"Bad is a relative term when it comes to this situation. I'll see you at 12. You know what, make that 11. I'm going to take an early lunch and you can be a potential client. You own your salon, it's plausible."

"Telling tales on the clock? Yeah, this is something serious. I'm going so I can call Cheyenne. See you at 11. Try not to come unglued before then, okay?"

"Okay, I'll try. Bye." Ember hit the off button on her phone and glanced at the clock on the wall. It was just after 10. She looked over at her computer and realized she hadn't even turned it on yet. She hit the button on the front and silently stared at the screen as it loaded, her mind elsewhere. She knew she wasn't going to get any real work done, but she could go through her email and note the ones she needed to reply to when she got back from lunch. She clicked the desktop icon for her email and watched while the messages populated. One immediately caught her eye. It had been sent five minutes ago and was from Cole. Her breathing quickened and she mentally told herself to get a grip. She was almost annoyed at the fact that even when he wasn't around, he was wreaking havoc on her senses. She clicked to open the email and read the contents.

"Ms. Sinclair, I hope you had a good holiday. I just spoke with Warren and he said you accepted his invitation to the cruise. I think this is a wonderful opportunity to gain firsthand experience of what we are trying to advertise. Since this is a work-related trip, you do not need to use any vacation time. I had planned to return to the office tomorrow, but in light of our impending trip I won't be returning until after the cruise. I would like to meet with you sometime during the first day of our trip to discuss our top three pitches. That way we have a working plan going in and we can tailor them to what we come across in our travels. Also, I know this trip has come up unexpectedly and you may have loose ends to tie up. After you handle any necessary office work for your impending time off, please take the rest of the day off today and the entire day tomorrow. I will see you on Thursday in South Carolina. Safe travels."

Ember hit the reply button and typed out a message thanking Cole for the time off and telling him that she would arrive in South Carolina prepared for their meeting. After she hit send on her message, she reread his message and found herself disappointed that he had called her Ms. Sinclair. Yet, wasn't that what she wanted? To go back to the way it was before they had indulged on Friday? Ember shook her head to get rid of the question, not wanting to try to answer it at that moment.

She activated her out of office reply on her email, shut her computer down, checked the remaining few messages on her work phone, changed her voicemail greeting to reflect her time off, and grabbed her things to go. She breezed by Cecile's desk, letting her know she was out for the rest of the day and tomorrow and got on the elevator. She would send Cecile an email about her impending trip so she could avoid the 1000 questions she knew she would be bombarded with. She just hoped that the office gossips would view this trip just like any other business trip anyone took. They had no reason to see it otherwise, right?

It was just after 10:30 when Ember stepped out of the building. Beasley's was only a few blocks away, and she would arrive early for her lunch date with Cheyenne and Gabriella but she would use that time to start making a list of all the things she needed to do and buy before she left for the cruise in just a few days.

Chapter Nine

"Let me get this straight, you were gifted with a seven day tropical cruise *and* the woman you are trying to pursue is going along too? How does your luck always run golden?" Micah said leaning against the kitchen counter, shaking his head at his eldest brother's good fortune.

"I don't know but I could sure use the vacation. Having Ember on the trip too is a definite plus," Cole mused as he leaned against the doorway to his parent's kitchen.

"Doesn't matter whether she's there or not if she isn't interested in a relationship with you," Rock said, drinking straight out of the orange juice carton.

"Who said anything about a relationship? What happens on the cruise stays on the cruise. They could play the seven day version of seven minutes in heaven. Man, I miss that game. Good times, good times," Micah said smiling at his memories.

"It's what happens in Vegas, not a cruise, Micah and Rock I hope you plan to finish the rest of that orange juice with your nasty ass," Onyx said, rolling her eyes after receiving a middle finger from her second oldest brother. "And again, a simple discussion about where the two of you want to take this will benefit you both, Cole."

"See, I still don't even think that's necessary. She wants you; you know that for damn sure. Instead of doing all that womanly talking, why not just use the ancient art of seduction. You two are about to be on a Caribbean cruise for fucks sake. Hot sun, bathing suits, beaches . . . do you see where I'm going with this?" Micah said as he eyed Cole.

"Yeah man, I got you. This does change the game a bit. I mean, it's one thing to try to do this locally where anyone from the office could see us if we go out together. It's another thing to be on a cruise ship where no one knows us and have a fling. This might actually be just what the doctor ordered."

"So, are you trying to date her or what?" Rock said, tossing the orange juice carton into the trash.

"Truthfully, no. After what I went through with Denise, dating isn't even on my radar. You date with the intent to build something with someone. The only thing I'm interested in building is business. Any relationship I have with a woman would be purely physical. Of course, I'm always up front with the women I see; they know the deal. But even that would be complicated with Ember since she works for me. A Caribbean fling would be best, honestly. No strings attached, we'd get each other out of our systems, and still work together after the trip is over." *There*, Cole thought, *I've made my decision. Now to get Ember on board with it.*

"Famous last words. I put money on it that it gets complicated and one of you catches feelings," Rock said with a challenge in his gray eyes.

"I'll take that bet," Micah said. "I've seen many short term flings work out and no feelings get involved."

"Yeah, they were all yours Black Casanova," Rock said. "And you think they worked out well but I bet you any of those women would have taken it further if they thought you wanted them to."

"Nope. Not the women I deal with. They know the score from the jump and they are fine with the arrangement," he said, taking a sip of the water he just poured.

"And you can also rent them by the hour," Onyx quipped, causing Micah to spit his water out and their two older brothers to howl with laughter.

* * *

"Ay dios mio," Gabriella said after Ember told her friends about her upcoming trip.

"Right. This is a comedy of freaking errors and I'm at the center of the joke," Ember said, as she sighed and looked down into her plate of chicken and waffles.

"I don't see the problem. In fact, I see a solution. Girl, go on this trip, have you a nice little fling and then get back to the work thing when you get back. You deserve to enjoy yourself. From what you've said about him, Cole will have no problem helping you enjoy yourself," Cheyenne said wiggling her thick but well maintained eyebrows suggestively.

"Absolutely out of the question," Ember said as she shook her head at Cheyenne's one-track mind. "Do you think about anything besides sex?"

"Sure. I think about . . . um . . . nope, sex might be it," Cheyenne admitted and Gabriella burst out laughing.

"We know Cheyenne is all about the sex, but it may not be such a bad idea," Gabriella admitted, pouring more honey on her chicken.

"Not you too! In what world is sleeping with your boss a good idea?" Ember demanded and then stuffed a piece of waffle in her mouth.

"A world where you lay down ground rules and go into the situation with your eyes open. Before you are boss and employee, you are a man and a woman. Y'all are obviously attracted to each other. You are about to be on a ship, in the middle of the ocean, with no one who knows you. How is this not perfect?" Cheyenne asked.

"The client knows us."

"You said the client is Cole's frat brother. You have nothing to worry about there. Frat bruhs don't break the code. No one will ever know," Cheyenne assured her.

"She's right about that," Gabriella confirmed.

"How do y'all even know that?" Ember asked.

"Because we did more than go to class and study in college," Cheyenne quipped.

"I think I'm offended," Ember said with a pout.

"You can be offended all you want, but you know it's the truth," Cheyenne said and then popped a piece of chicken in her mouth.

"I can't with you right now," Ember said to Cheyenne and then turned her attention to Gabriella. "Gab, why on earth are you cosigning with Cheyenne of all people? I thought you had good sense."

"I think I'm offended now but I don't even care because this peach soda is making everything okay. Carry on," Cheyenne said as she sipped her soda.

Gabriella laughed at Cheyenne and then turned to Ember. "I agree with Chey. As long as you both go into this arrangement knowing it's short term and nothing will come of it, I think it's fine. You two obviously have chemistry and I can't remember the last time you mentioned your sex life. Not since that guy you dated for a while after undergrad. That was what, around two or three years ago? And I can't remember if you even slept with him."

"I did. Once. It was about as memorable as the two guys in college," Ember said rolling her eyes.

"Then I think you're way overdue. It seems like your fairy godmother or fate has dropped this opportunity in your lap and you'd be crazy not to take it. There's no guesswork, no awkward dates where you try to figure out where this is going. You know what you both want and you can get down to business. If it was me, I'd go in with a list of fantasies and make sure I covered all of them."

"But I would still have to see him after the trip was over."

"Maybe, but you admitted that before you started working on this client together you two were never around each other and you admired him from afar. Once the trip is over and the client makes a decision, you won't see him on a daily or probably even weekly basis. And you don't plan to stay there a lot longer either. Before you know it you'll be moving on and starting your own firm. Who knows when another opportunity like this will drop in your lap? I want to be clear, if this was my situation, I wouldn't hesitate," Gabriella admitted and then took a sip of her sweet tea.

"If I promise to think about it, can we drop it for now? I need to get my life together, shop for things I need to take with me, pack, figure out where I'm going to leave my car in Charleston . . ."

"I hope you know we are escorting you down to South Carolina so we can get a up close glimpse of this dude, so that's one thing off your to do list. If he's as fine as you act like he is, I need to see it with my own eyes," Cheyenne warned.

"I'm down. Road trip!" Gabriella agreed.

"Shit, let's leave today and have a girl's trip down in Charleston. Ember you can shop for your trip and we can help you not show up looking like someone's momma."

"You offend me one more time today and I'll kick your ass all the way down to Charleston," Ember warned.

"That'll be the day. Let's roll out," Cheyenne said and they left to get packed and get on the road.

Chapter Ten

Ember was conflicted as she stepped out of the car, smoothed out her pink and white sundress, and retrieved her luggage from the trunk. She stared at the beautiful ship in front of her and was immediately excited about the much-needed trip she was about to embark on. The weather in Charleston was clear and according to weather forecasts, it was going to remain that way the entire time they were on the cruise. Her excitement was dampened just a bit by the worry she felt about seeing Cole again. It had been almost a week since their encounter in the meeting room and, despite Cheyenne and Gabriella doing their best to convince her that she should have a fling with him, she hadn't made a decision.

Ember was honestly shocked that she was even considering it but Cheyenne and Gabriella had made some very good arguments about why she should take advantage of this chance. Much of the last few days had been spent engaging in girl talk and buying clothing for the trip. Although she thought her clothes were beautiful and classy, they were definitely not cruise ship appropriate and given that this trip was very last minute, she didn't have a choice but to purchase new things. Since Charleston was a cruise port, many of the shops carried clothes for cruising and she found quite a bit to choose from. She had indulged in new sundresses, shorts, tank tops, and two gorgeous formal gowns for the captain's dinner. Although there was only one captain's dinner, she wanted to have a choice. Cheyenne and Gabriella had even convinced her to buy new lingerie, although she suspected they had ulterior motives for that.

"I can't wait to see Mr. Fine CEO up close and personal," Cheyenne said, joining Ember at the trunk.

"You promised you wouldn't cut up. Don't renig now Chey," Ember requested.

"If you believed that promise, then I have some swampland in Mississippi to sell you. Prime real estate, I promise," Gabriella said, joining her two friends behind the car.

"I'm not renigging heffas," Cheyenne promised. "I said I wouldn't cut up in front of *him*. I don't see *him* anywhere in sight. When *he* gets here, I will be on my best behavior."

The trio heard a masculine "ahem" and then an equally masculine chuckle. They turned simultaneously and found themselves staring at three of the best looking men they had ever seen. They looked alike, but each man was sexy in his own way. It was clear they were related and Ember assumed the two men with Cole were his brothers.

"Good morning Mr. Bainbridge," Ember said, meeting his eyes and trying to calm her rapidly beating heart, which had just betrayed her by jumping into her throat.

"Come on, we're about to go cruising. Surely you can call me Cole," Cole requested with a smile, hoping to ease the awkward tension flowing between them.

"Yes, of course, Cole," Ember said as she returned Cole's smile, her cheeks warming at the thought of what happened the last time he asked her to call him Cole.

"Ho-ly shit," Cheyenne sighed. Gabriella elbowed her as Ember cut her eyes toward her, only to notice that Cheyenne wasn't looking at Cole, but rather the man standing on his left, whose gray eyes were staring back at her with mild agitation. *Well, at least it wasn't directed at Cole*, Ember thought.

"Hi, I'm Micah, Cole's brother." The man without gray eyes said. "On the other side of Cole is a neighborhood kid we took in to keep him off the streets," Micah joked, reaching out to shake Gabriella's hand.

"Gabriella. And this is Cheyenne and Ember," Gabriella said grasping Micah's hand and giving it a firm shake. She couldn't help but laugh at the description he gave of his brother.

"If that's what neighborhood kids look like around your way, I need your address immediately," Cheyenne requested, much to Ember's embarrassment. *Renigging heffa*, Ember thought to herself.

"I'm Rock. Ignore my younger brother; mom dropped him on the head quite a few times when he was a baby. She was pretty tired by the time he came around," Rock disclosed as he shook each woman's hand, noticing that Cheyenne held on a bit longer than the other two ladies.

"What time do you board the ship?" Gabriella asked Ember, seeing that Cheyenne was well on her way to getting out of hand.

"Not for another 45 minutes or so. I guess we all got here a bit too early," Ember replied as she consulted her watch.

"Cole is early for everything. Except holiday visits. He's a whole day late for them," Micah said with a smirk. If looks could kill, the one he got from Cole surely would have had him dead and buried.

Sensing his life was in danger, Micah quickly changed the subject. "How about a drink before you two shove off? That café over there is advertising brunch cocktails."

"It's barely noon," Gabriella said.

"It's cocktail hour somewhere in the universe; we just need to pretend that we're there," Micah replied.

"I'm down for a drink," Cheyenne said.

"What's new?" Ember countered and Gabriella busted out laughing.

"I'm gonna act like I didn't hear that," Cheyenne replied as she started walking towards the café and the others followed.

"Play deaf all you want, you know I'm right," Ember said as she blew Cheyenne a kiss and side stepped the left hook that Cheyenne pretended to throw at her.

"You better be glad I dodged that. I would've had to mollywop you," Ember warned Cheyenne.

"Eh, you hit like a bitch anyway so . . ." Cheyenne countered.

"You just really don't know what public behavior is, do you Chey? Loud cussing ass," Gabriella said.

"Says the fool who just called her an ass out in public," Ember said hollering with laughter.

"Oh damn." Gabriella said when she realized her error, making Ember laugh even harder.

Cole was intrigued by the Ember that he was seeing today. He had never been around her outside of work. No one in the office would call her uptight or boring, but she did remain professional at all times. Seeing her in chill mode with her friends added another facet to her personality, one that Cole was quickly growing to like.

After a round of margaritas and small talk Rock asked, "So how long have you three known each other?"

"We've been best friends since freshman year of college, inseparable ever since," Cheyenne answered.

"Kind of like the three musketeers, huh?" Micah laughed.

"There were four of us; we lost one," Cheyenne said. Realizing what she had just said, she quickly took a drink as she felt sadness wash over her.

Recognizing that the mood was about to turn somber, Micah said, "Well, I've known these two losers for almost 34 years. I've tried to get rid of them a few times but none of my plans worked."

"That's because you were one of mom's bad eggs, baby brother. If it had been me, I would have easily taken you both out. You'd do well to remember that," Rock warned.

"Picture me being worried about you. Wait, you can't," Micah laughed.

"Tall, dark, and sinister huh Rock? Just the way I like them," Cheyenne said, staring him directly into his gray eyes.

"Just the way she likes them Rock," Micah mimicked. "And how do you like them, Ember?" Micah asked, which won him another deadly look from Cole.

"Ember, I'm more than ready to leave these jokers and get on the ship. Are you ready to head out?" Cole asked, shaking his head at his brothers' antics.

"I'm more than ready as well, especially since my best friend seems to have left her public behavior in the car," Ember said eyeing Cheyenne. Cole paid for the group's drinks and they walked back to the cars.

"Bye you two. Gab, take her home," Ember said as she hugged Gabriella. When she leaned in to hug her, Cheyenne warned, "Ember if you don't sleep with that gorgeous man I'm going to disown you." Ember sincerely hoped Cole hadn't heard Cheyenne's barely whispered words.

Cole had heard Cheyenne and silently thanked her for once again letting him know that Ember had been talking about him and whatever this was between them. He owed that woman a present or something. He said bye to his brothers and then picked up his bag in one hand and Ember's in the other.

"Ready?" he asked.

"Yes," Ember responded.

As they walked toward the ship, Ember looked back to see Gabriella tugging Cheyenne's arm and motioning her to the car. Ember wished her luck because Cheyenne often had a one-track mind and right now Cole's brother Rock was receiving all of her focus.

Chapter Eleven

Ember sat her bag down on the bed and looked around her huge cabin. Bold hues of gold, pink, and orange created a warm and inviting feel in the room but they made Ember feel sensual and powerful too. Her thoughts on sensuality immediately turned to Cole. Seeing him with his brothers made him a real person to her, not just her boss. He had remained chill while his brothers had joked around, and Ember suspected that was how it typically was and not because they had been in the company of ladies. Although she was an only child, she knew people who were the oldest of their siblings and they were typically more reserved and responsible. This afternoon had been the first time she had been around Cole in a non-professional setting and she had enjoyed it. She had caught him looking at her a few times but she couldn't fault him for that since the reason she had caught him was because she was stealing looks at him.

Were Cheyenne and Gabriella right?

Should she take this opportunity for what it was and enjoy herself for the first time in a long time? Or should she not risk the possible complications that sleeping with Cole could cause? While Cheyenne and Gabriella had a point that in theory this could be the perfect opportunity, she also had to take into consideration that they had professions where engaging in an affair with a boss or supervisor would not be a possible career-ending choice. Cheyenne was a photographer and had relationships with quite a few magazines and newspapers, but she was essentially her own boss. Gabriella owned her own salon and only answered to the owner of the building where she operated her salon. In fact, Gabriella had never even met the owner of the building. She had signed her lease through a lawyer.

In Ember's case, if it got out that she slept with her boss, she would be branded as a woman who used sex to climb the corporate ladder. If the affair went sour with Cole and she had to leave, if she had a reputation for sleeping with her boss, the next boss might expect the same. There was the option of starting her own company if all else failed, but she had a plan and she wanted to stick to it. She sighed deeply. She knew that one day, when she was at the head of the most successful advertising agency owned by a woman of color, the sacrifice would be worth it. Wouldn't it? She was beginning to think not.

* * *

Cole looked around his cabin and he had to admit he was impressed. The brochures and promotional material he had seen were nice, but they didn't do the real thing justice. The huge king sized bed, big bathroom with a Jacuzzi jet tub and a small but nicely stocked efficiency kitchen were definitely nice. There was also a table big enough for two right under the large porthole window. The outlets and telephone on the table indicated that it could be used for both dining and as a work desk. The color scheme of the room was earth tones, which Cole felt was a nice change from the usual blue and gray nautical themes you found on most cruise ships. Browns, reds, and oranges gave the cabin a comfortable, homey feel. He wondered if Ember's cabin was the same or if hers had a different theme.

Ember.

Cheyenne's whispered request clearly let him know that he she had been discussing him. Luckily his brothers didn't have loose lips like Cheyenne, since he liked to always be the one with the upper hand. Ember calling him Mr. Bainbridge earlier made him wonder if she planned to ignore her friend's request. They'd made small talk as they boarded the ship and made their way toward their rooms but she seemed a bit standoffish, almost like she had something on her mind. He hoped it was him. Cole didn't mind using his charms to convince her that they should indulge in the time and space they had together, but it would be so much easier if she was all in from the gate. It would definitely maximize their time. Seven nights was a perfect time frame for a fling and he didn't want to waste one moment. Once their time was up, they would have to decide if they wanted to carry on with the affair. He would make sure that she understood that it could be nothing more than an affair, whether it lasted 7 days or 7 months. He still stood by his decision to protect his heart and his money. The one time he had failed to protect himself, he had almost lost half of everything he owned.

Cole still felt a pang of anger when he thought of how Denise had played him so well, almost expertly. He met her at a charity gala. He was there to support a children's hospital; she was there to find a rich husband. Cole had been weary of her at first; having met many women who were clearly gold diggers put him on constant alert. But then she donated $10,000 of her own money to the charity and disclosed that she was an heiress to. Denise had told Cole over drinks that she was an only child and her parents had been killed in a plane crash when she was four. Her parents had been only children and her paternal grandparents, who recently passed away, raised her. She presented herself as a beautiful, educated, philanthropist who wanted to make the world a better place. Cole fell for it hook, line, and sinker. Less than a year later they were engaged. His family broached the topic of a prenuptial agreement, which Cole was honestly on the fence about. He felt that if he planned to spend his life with this woman, his money would be spending it too. Not to mention the fact that she was wealthy in her own right. Yet, he knew his family wouldn't steer him wrong, so he broached the subject. She went ballistic and threatened to call the wedding off. This set bells off in Rock's head and he dug into Denise's past. After calling in a few favors, Rock discovered that Denise was not wealthy at all and instead was from a middle class family in southern California. Both of her parents were still living and she worked as an online humanities instructor. The $10,000 Cole had seen her donate had been part of a $50,000 loan she had taken out to perpetuate an affluent lifestyle in an effort to capture a rich husband. And she had almost done it. Her family was in on it; her parents cosigned for the loan. Cole swore off committed relationships of any kind and spent the last 10 years as a confirmed bachelor. He had absolutely no intention of changing that now

Cole could feel the ship begin to move and realized that they must be officially under way. It was just after 3:00pm and dinner was served at 5:30pm. He and Ember would be having dinner with Warren Drake and his business partner James Franklin. The ad team that Cole and Ember were up against would also be at this dinner and Cole was itching to get a look at the competition. Just before they separated to go to their rooms, he and Ember had made plans to meet after dinner to discuss the other team and choose the top three pitches they wanted to develop while on the cruise. That way they could be mindful of pitch points as they enjoyed the amenities and excursions. Cole yawned and decided that he needed to be on his A Game for this dinner meeting and a quick power nap was probably a good idea. He also needed his rest, since he planned to be up all hours of the night with Ember, starting tonight.

Chapter Twelve

Cole was seated at the table eyeing the competition. His parents had ingrained in him that to be early was to be on time and to be on time was to be late, so he had arrived early, intent on being the first one at the table so that he would have the upper hand when choosing seating. It was 5:25 and everyone had arrived except Ember. He was making small talk with Warren about the upcoming NFL season and what chance the Panthers had at a win when Warren's face changed from amusement to masculine appreciation. Cole turned and saw Ember making her way to the table. Damn she looked good. *Hell, she always looks good* he thought as he and the other men at the table stood as she took her seat next to him. But this was a different kind of good. This was an outfit that she would have never worn to work and he was really starting to enjoy her non-work persona.

Ember decided that she had chosen the right outfit for tonight if the look on Cole's face was any indication. Her golden yellow tank top dipped just low enough in the front to be acceptable for a dinner meeting but her back was completely out. Her red and orange striped maxi skirt accentuated her figure without being too overt. She had piled her ebony curls on her head and pinned them into a loose bun. Her make up was done to perfection, complete with her winged eyeliner and her signature lip gloss. She looked and felt like a Caribbean goddess. Cole pulled out her chair and she brushed against him slightly as she sat down. The contact was slight enough that no one else at the table had noticed but if the sharp intake of breath Cole had taken was any indication, he had. There were butterflies in her stomach and they were flying around in the anticipation that she was feeling.

"Ms. Sinclair, as beautiful as always. So glad you could join us," Warren said as she got herself settled at the table.

"Thank you Mr. Drake and please call me Ember. Again thank you for inviting us on this trip. Everything is beautiful. I can't wait to get into the casino and relax in the spa," Ember replied.

"Please, call me Warren. And you are more than welcome; I hope you enjoy everything and don't forget to check out a few excursions. Unfortunately a family emergency called my partner, Joseph, away and he won't be joining us on this trip. This is Allen James and Vincent Green from Foster Glenn Advertising," Warren said, indicating the men sitting at the table with them.

"Good evening gentlemen," Ember greeted them.

"Good evening," The two men replied at the same time. Cole wasn't so pleased with the way Vincent's gaze lingered on Ember during the introductions. The blatant male appreciation he saw in Vincent's eyes set his teeth on edge. He briefly questioned why he had such a strong reaction, but quickly decided the only answer could be that he wanted to be on the receiving end of Ember's attention during this trip and he wasn't interested in sharing it with anyone. That had to be it; to consider anything else was unacceptable.

"Cole, are you with us?" Warren asked. Hearing his name jarred him out of his thoughts and set him on edge even more because he had been caught slipping.

"I just had an idea for an ad and was running it through my mind. You know I'm always thinking," he offered, hoping that would serve to explain him being lost in his thoughts and put the competition on notice that he was in the game. He locked eyes with Ember and she seemed interested in what he had been thinking about. *Well, at least I fooled her,* he thought.

"Is it Mrs. or Miss. Sinclair, if you don't mind me asking? I want to make sure I address you correctly." Realizing that she was being addressed, Ember reluctantly broke eye contact with Cole to respond to Vincent.

"It's Miss. But please, call me Ember," she replied.

"Gladly, and please call me Vinny. Ember is a unique name. I've never met anyone with it before," Vinny said, obviously inquiring about the origin of Ember's name.

"My mother named me. She wanted me to have a strong name, but she also wanted it to be unique. She chose Ember because when you try to put a fire out, the strongest part is the embers. They hold on and refuse to be extinguished and they often restart the fire despite efforts to put it out. Mom had a way with words," Ember explained with a bittersweet smile. She'd never get over the pain of losing her mother, but she had gotten to the point where she could remember her mother without feeling the sharp pain of loss.

Cole remembered when Ember lost her father; she had been working for the firm for a couple of years when he'd died and he remembered the staff getting together to send flowers and a card. He hadn't known that she lost her mother as well. She must have died before Ember began working for him. He felt a stab of pain for her, knowing that he would be devastated if he lost one of his parents and here she had lost both. His sympathy turned to acute agitation when he heard Vinny addressing Ember again.

"Restarting a fire is impressive indeed," Vinny said with a smile. Ember hoped she was imagining it, but it seemed that

Vinny was openly flirting. He was nice looking enough, with his mocha colored skin, deep chocolate eyes, and muscular build but he was no Cole. Not even close. He was too flashy, with his huge gold watch and bracelet to match. His clothes were obviously expensive but in a gaudy way. *Could men be gaudy?* Ember wondered. Well, if they could, Vinny was the poster child for it. And she didn't like the way he was clearly flirting with her. This was supposed to be a business meeting. Didn't he have any business decorum? She wasn't feeling him at all. However, she didn't want to come off as bitchy, especially since she was the only woman at the table. And she didn't want Warren to think that she was an overemotional woman. That was a death sentence in this industry. It was best to just play it cool and polite.

"It seems I'm last to join the table. Were you all talking about anything interesting?" she asked, hoping to divert Vinny's attention elsewhere.

"Well, Cole was trying to convince me that the Panthers have a chance in hell of making it to the playoffs this season," Warren answered with an unconvinced smirk on his face.

"I'm telling you, you're going to eat those words," Cole warned. "My boys have been making some major moves and I think we're about to see some big changes from them."

"I don't know Warren, Cole might have a point. The Panthers made some serious offensive changes this year. They drafted a new tight end, Price is his name I think, and made other changes on their offensive line. Plus they extended Newton's contract, which keeps experience and leadership in the locker room. Those moves are key in changing the Panthers from no chance in hell to going all the way. They still can't hold a flame to my Colts, but that could make them a close second," Ember interjected and then took a sip of her water. She looked around at the stunned faces of the men sitting at the table and smiled slightly around her glass. In addition to being a true football fan, she knew she had to be well versed in male-dominated subjects if she was going to stay competitive in a male-dominated field.

"You're a sports fan, I see," Warren said, the first to recover his voice. Ember thought she detected a hint of approval in his eyes. *Good*, she thought, *that will earn us some points.*

"Oh yes. I never miss a Colts game. I catch most of the Panthers games too. I figure I should stay up on them since I'm technically a North Carolinian," she laughed. Out of the corner of her eye she saw Cole eyeing her with that intense look again.

"A woman who's beautiful and likes sports? Can you cook and balance a budget? If so . . ." Vincent trailed off and started to laugh. Clearly he saw his comment as a compliment. Ember decided she didn't like him. She gave him a forced smile and turned her attention back to Warren.

Cole decided he was not a fan of Vinny. He was clearly flirting with Ember and Cole didn't like it at all. A surge of jealousy quickly shot though him and just as quickly he told it to take a hike. Ember wasn't his woman and she was free to talk to whomever she wanted, right? But the thought of Ember with any man but him made Cole want to karate chop someone in the throat. What the hell was wrong with him? He needed to get it together because this was not the Cole way of doing things.

There was one thing Vinny was right about; Cole was learning quickly that Ember was indeed the full package: smart, successful, beautiful, funny and liked sports. Although she didn't answer Vinny when he inquired about her cooking and budgeting, Cole was willing to wager that she was a good cook. Word around the office was that she was partial to baking and would often bring baked goods in for her coworkers. Although her salary wouldn't make her rich by any means, he knew she earned a decent amount of money. She didn't seem like the type to spend frivolously.

Cole felt like he was being watched and looked up to see a waiter looking at him expectedly. *Dammit*, he thought, *I zoned out again. What the hell is wrong with me tonight?*

"Thinking of another idea for an ad, Cole?" Warren asked with a smirk and twinkle in his eye.

"I'm always thinking of a master plan," Cole confidently replied and then turned his attention back to the waiter. "Would you mind repeating that?" he asked.

"No problem sir. Tonight we have three entrees to choose from. First, we have pork loins smothered in cranberry gravy with scalloped potatoes and julienned root vegetables. If that is not to your liking, we also have an 8 oz. top sirloin steak with mashed red potatoes and sautéed green beans. Finally, we have a Caribbean jerk chicken served with curry potatoes and fried asparagus. What would you like tonight, sir?"

"Well, my choices are limited because I don't eat pork or beef, so it's a good thing I love jerk chicken." Cole said with a smile that changed to a look of confusion when Warren and Allen chuckled and Ember raised an inquisitive eyebrow. "What?" he asked.

"You could have just said 'Ditto to what she said and I'll have what she's having' and saved us from having to hear the menu again," Vinny said and smiled, though the smile didn't quite meet his eyes.

Cole's eyes swung to meet Ember's and her eyebrow was still raised. "What did I do?" he asked her.

"You literally repeated exactly what I said a few moments ago. I don't eat pork or beef either and also ordered the jerk chicken. I can't wait to hear these ideas that you're getting," Ember said and chuckled. He looked a bit embarrassed and she wondered what had him so distracted.

"I guess we work so well together, we don't even know when we're working together," Cole countered, hoping to make light of the situation.

"Indeed," Ember said laughing again.

"So Allen, how long have you two worked together?" Cole asked, getting back to his initial goal at this dinner, which was to size up the competition.

"We opened Foster Glenn roughly ten years ago. The rest is, as they say, history," Allen responded with a flick of the wrist. From his response Ember could see that Allen was as conceited as his partner was gaudy. Interesting combination.

"Your last names are James and Green, where did you come up with the name Foster Glenn?" Ember asked.

"Our fathers were brothers. We named the company after their first names," Vinny replied.

"Ah, you two are cousins; it's a family affair," Cole observed.

"Yes and how did you two come up with Commercial Innovations? Very catchy. Are you two related as well?" Vinny said, although he looked less than impressed with the name and more interested in the part Cole played in Ember's life.

"Oh no, we aren't partners," Ember responded. "Cole is my boss."

"Ember is one of my best senior ad executives and we are working together on this project. I chose the name because when I was growing up, my favorite part of watching tv was the commercials. My company takes commercials to the next level, hence the use of the word innovations," Cole explained coolly. Vinny was beginning to annoy him.

"Interesting," was all Vinny offered back in a response before he turned his attention back to Ember. He looked like he was about to ask her a question, when the waiter arrived with their food and talking took a back seat to eating.

Chapter Thirteen

After dinner and dessert had been eaten and thoroughly enjoyed, Warren invited everyone to the dance deck where a live band was playing salsa music. Ember had loved salsa dancing ever since Gabriella had taught her, Cheyenne, and Violet how to do it during their sophomore year in college. She hadn't been salsa dancing in at least a year and was genuinely excited to get on the dance floor. When they arrived on the dance deck, she thought that she was going to be forced to politely decline a dance offer from Vinny but he loudly announced that salsa dancing wasn't his thing and he planned to enjoy watching everyone else dance. Relieved, Ember turned her attention to the dance floor and began tapping her foot to the beat.

"Cole, I think you may want to take Ember out on the floor before I have to replace the part of the floor she's tapping her foot on," Warren called out to him with a laugh.

"I think you might be right," he called back, laughing himself. Ember had caught the exchange and nodded her head yes when Cole asked if she would like to dance. As they walked out to the floor she wondered if she should feel nervous about dancing with him but before any nerves could kick in, Cole reached out, captured her arm, and spun her around. Before she knew it they were salsa dancing like they had been partners for years. For some reason it surprised her that he was so good at it. He was always so business-focused that it never occurred to her that he had outside interests. And man, could he dance.

Their bodies moved to the beat as one and Cole wondered if this was an indication of how well they would move together under the sheets. Even if it took him the entire time they were on the ship he was damned well determined to find out. The times that her body briefly pressed against his, electric shocks that he swore were visible to the naked eye had radiated from his body. After their third straight dance, Ember indicated that she needed a drink. Although he didn't want to stop dancing with her, he had to admit that between the dancing and the warmer climate that the ship had moved into, he needed a drink himself. As they made their way back to where they had left the others, Cole saw Vinny staring at them. The look in his eyes was clear displeasure and Cole wondered again if the sparks between him and Ember were visible. It was such a ridiculous notion, yet he could see that Vinny had seen something between them that he didn't like.

"You two looked professional out there," Warren remarked as they took their seats and Cole motioned for the waitress to bring them some water. "I might need to hire you to dance in one of our commercials," he joked.

"We come free with a purchased ad package," Ember replied with a mischievous smile. Warren threw his head back and laughed. Allen and Vinny were not nearly as amused.

"We are going to head over to the casino. Anyone care to join us?" Allen asked.

"I have early morning meetings and probably need to head on to my room actually," Warren said.

"Now that I'm sitting still, I'm a little tired," Ember announced. "I think I might just turn in for the night myself."

"I'd be glad to escort you to your room Ember," Vinny said with a smile that indicated he'd like to do more than just escort her. Before she could reply, Cole chimed in.

"Don't trouble yourself. I'll escort her. I need to get some papers from her and this would be as good a time as any to get them," Cole said tersely and Vinny's face reflected controlled agitation. Ember watched the pissing contest between the two men with amused indignation. Although she was grateful for the bail out, she certainly didn't need an escort and was perfectly capable of walking to her room alone.

"Wouldn't be any trouble at all. Maybe another night when you don't have to work Ember," Vinny replied and then he and Allen said their goodbyes and left.

"On that note, I will see you two tomorrow. It's a day at sea so try some of our ship activities. I'm sure you'll find something to enjoy," Warren said with a smile that Cole recognized all too well. He hoped Ember had missed it.

"Night Warren," Cole said to his back as he walked away. "Ready?" he asked Ember. She nodded yes and they began to make their way to the area of the ship where the cabins were housed. They made small talk about the parts of the ship they passed but in the back of Ember's mind she was trying to decide what she should do when they reached her door. She knew Cole had fed Vinny a line about the papers, so that wasn't something they needed to discuss. Should she invite him in and have "the talk"? She had genuinely enjoyed herself this evening and she hated to end the night with telling Cole they would not be intimate. She stifled a yawn and continued to think. She hadn't lied about being tired but if he was still interested in her, tonight would be the best night to talk and set an understanding for the rest of the trip. She certainly didn't want this feeling of the unknown hanging over her as she tried to enjoy herself this week. And then, just like that, they were at her cabin door.

They stood outside the door in a slightly awkward silence, each trying to decide how to approach the other. Now that Ember was faced with a moment of truth, she found that she didn't want to remain platonic and she most certainly didn't want Cole to keep his distance. She wanted to sleep with him. They locked eyes simultaneously and silently decided that no more time would be wasted. Cole knew he should pause and make sure she understood the terms that he brought to the table, but he couldn't think past the need to be inside of her in some way. Ember slid her plastic door key into the slot, opened the door, walked through, and motioned for Cole to follow. The door closed behind him and she briefly reopened it to slide the "do not disturb" sign on the outside doorknob. She turned back around and he was right there, staring at her with that intense look again. This time she knew she wasn't imagining it.

She locked eyes with him and reached out to wrap her hand around his tie. Slowly she pulled him in and, for one of the first times in his adult life, Cole gladly followed. When their faces were nano inches away from each other, Ember licked her top lip and then leaned in and did the same to his. In one fluid motion he pinned her to the door with his body, leaning in and grinding against her while sealing their mouths in a kiss. Never had a woman made him want her more. He knew right then and there that their first time together wasn't going to be in a bed but rather right up against that door. He reached in between their bodies, undid his pants and then shrugged out of his suit jacket, never breaking their kiss. She followed his lead and pulled up her skirt, uncovering the thin black lace panties she was wearing. She tried unsuccessfully to slide them down her legs and sensing her trouble, he broke the kiss to slide them down for her. On the way back up he paused to push his pants and boxer briefs down his legs and then leaned in to whisper in her ear.

"I need to be inside of you."

Warmth flooded her body and she responded to his request by wrapping her leg around him; it was an invitation for him to enter. He grabbed her other leg and wrapped it around him on the other side, using the door as leverage to hold her up. His manhood was right at her opening, and as he began to slide in she moaned at the delicious pressure of him entering her. She was so tight around him that he almost mistook her for a virgin.

Until she started to move.

She was using her core muscles and the wall to move up and down on his shaft. It was a maximum power play and she was once again in control. He braced himself against her as she rode him in midair like some kind of bewitching goddess, the look of absolute bliss playing across her face. Her body milked him and intense waves of pleasure cashed over him. He was losing control in more ways than one and he had to take back the reins of power before he completely lost his mind. He moved his arms to her hips, clasped his hands around her back, and began to move in and out of her, trapping her tighter between him and the door with each thrust. She let him take over and each thrust pushed her a little closer to the edge until she fell into the deepest, most intense orgasm of her life. The feeling of her pulsing and tightening around him sent him plunging over the edge. She felt his release inside of her as he ground his head against her neck and groaned out his pleasure.

They slid to the floor, spent. She kept her legs wrapped around him and leaned over to put her forehead against his chest. They were a mess of tangled clothes, heavy breathing, and satisfied bodies. They stayed like that for a few minutes and then Cole noticed that Ember had become a little heavier than she initially was. He angled his head so that he could see her face and discovered that she had fallen asleep. She was out cold. This was the first time he had ever screwed a woman to sleep and a feeling of male pride surged through him.

He gently untangled their bodies, carefully laid her down on the floor and stood to straighten his clothes. He then gathered her into his arms and carried her to the bed. He thought about undressing her and putting her under the covers but that seemed a little creepy, so he just removed her shoes and made sure she was far enough on the bed that she wasn't in danger of falling off. He also decided against staying the night; she wasn't awake to invite him so he wouldn't presume that she wanted him there when she woke up in the morning. So that she wouldn't think he had bailed on her, he left a note on the table asking her to join him at breakfast. As the door closed behind him, he realized that they hadn't used any birth control. Never, ever had he been so careless. They had much to discuss in the morning.

Chapter Fourteen

Ember yawned, stretched, and rolled over to onto her back. She felt rested and relaxed and better than she had in months. Sunlight from the porthole streamed into the room, indicating that morning had come. She stretched once more and then decided she wanted just a little more rest. Just as she was falling back to sleep, she bolted up into a sitting position. She looked over at the door of her cabin, mainly because that's the last place she remembered being. Then she realized she was still fully clothed and laying on top of the covers. Ember never slept in clothes and rarely entertained a nightgown. Her clothes and the sore but satisfied feeling at her core let her know that the memories of last night that were quickly coming back to her were fact, rather than fiction. Wide awake now, she began to wonder if she was relieved or angry that she had woken up alone but quickly decided that she was relieved. She needed time to process everything and time to prepare to see Cole again. She needed to do what she did best: think.

Ember's stomach grumbled. First order of action was to eat. It was impossible for Ember to think on an empty stomach. She moved from the bed to the table to retrieve the room service menu and noticed a note on top of the menu with her name on it. Knowing it could only be from one person, she picked it up and opened the folded paper.

Breakfast? Brunch? Text me. —Cole

Ember picked up her cell phone and saw that it was just after nine. It would definitely be brunch or lunch and she would definitely eat breakfast before she met with him. She picked up the room service menu, quickly scanned it, and used the room phone to place her order. She then sent Cole a text that simply said "Lunch/brunch @12:30?" Almost immediately he responded with "Sounds good, casino café?" She agreed and then went to take a shower before her room service arrived.

Ember had just stepped out of the shower, wrapped herself in the plush robe hanging in the bathroom, and unpinned her hair when she heard a knock on her door. Impressed with the quickness of the ship's room service, she went to the door and swung it open.

Except room service was not on the other side. Vincent Green was.

"Ember, I must say that robe looks better on you than it does hanging on the back of the bathroom door. I have the same one in my room," Vinny said, appreciatively taking in Ember's attire.

"Thank you, I think. Was there something you needed Vinny?"

"Yes, of course. I don't have your number or I would have called. Would you like to join me for lunch? Just because we're competing for the same account doesn't mean we can't be friends, right?" It was clear that Vinny was trying to be charming, but it was lost on Ember because her first impression of him was a lasting one.

"Well, as you can see, I'm just getting up and I just ordered myself some breakfast. In fact, here it is coming up behind you," Ember explained, trying not to sound too dismissive.

Vinny looked behind him and saw a waiter pushing a cart down the hall in their direction and turned back to Ember, determination evident on his face. "Since you're having a late breakfast, maybe not lunch. Drinks and dinner?" he offered. Ember realized she was going to have to be a bit more obvious about saying no. Still, she didn't want to be rude—for a myriad of reasons. The waiter bringing her food in gave her a bit of time to think about how to word her rejection. By the time the waiter had been tipped and left, she thought she had a good response.

"Well, to be honest Vinny, I'm doing just what Warren advised us to do: treat this time like a vacation. So I'm not really making plans. I'm just doing what I feel, when I feel like it. You know? Vacation behavior," Ember explained, hoping he would get the point.

"Ah. I certainly understand that. Well, enjoy your breakfast. I do hope to be a part of your vacation behavior at some point this week. I'll see you later," Vinny said, sounding more like he was making a promise than a request. He took one last appreciative look at her standing there in her robe and then turned and started walking towards the elevators down the hall. Ember quickly shut her door and sat down to eat.

As she ate what had to be the best waffles she ever tasted, she honestly examined the situation. She wanted Cole; there was no doubt about that. The guesswork on trying to figure out if he wanted her had been taken out of the equation, first in the meeting room but definitely after last night. She reflected on the potential harm an affair with her boss could cause her career. If they kept the affair strictly to the ship and ended it once the cruise was over, she didn't have to worry about office gossip and her reputation. And if she was completely honest with herself, even if the affair went sour and she had to leave Commercial Innovations, she was more than able to move on to another company or start her own firm.

If she was still being honest with herself, her sex life was a disaster. She told herself that it didn't matter and that her ménage a mois would keep her going, but that was a lie and she knew it. She needed some two-person loving in the worst way. While she still stood by her decision that a relationship wasn't what she wanted at this time, she was woman enough to admit that she could use some good sex. And Cole definitely fell into the category of good sex. No, great sex.

"I need this, and for the moment I need him," Ember said out loud, needing to hear herself say it with her own ears.

Now, how to approach it? Should she just show up to lunch and lay everything out on the table? Or should she let him bring it up? Though her sexual experiences weren't much to be proud of, her line of work had taught her how to present a false persona. In advertising, you had to prove to the client that you were the most confident and the best equipped to handle their account. She knew enough about human nature that she could do this with Cole easily. But he came off as a man who wanted to be in charge and in control at all times. Maybe she should let him set their path. She thought about that for a moment. No, this was going to be about her. This was her show and he would need to figure out how to play along. If he played nice, she had some fantasies she wouldn't mind putting into action. She smiled, thinking how interesting the next six nights . . . and days . . . were going to be.

Chapter Fifteen

Cole had picked the most isolated booth in the casino's café. It was modeled after a 1950's soda shop, complete with a soda fountain, checkered floor, and juke box that played old love songs. At the moment, "You Make Me Feel Brand New" by the Stylistics was playing. Cole loved old school music and appreciated that both couples and families could enjoy the café's atmosphere. Personally, he wouldn't mind bringing Ember back here after dark to do some old school making out. It occurred to him that making out, or the insinuation of such, could be a strong marketing point for couples. He made a mental note to highlight that information in their pitch.

Just as "You Make Me Feel Brand New" went off and "Saturday Night Love" came on, Cole saw Ember walk in. She was wearing a simple yellow halter top and high-waisted dark blue shorts with white buttons on either side, black sandals, and her hair was piled on top of her hair in a curly afro puff. It was crazy how such a simple outfit could send his libido into overdrive. He liked the clothes she wore to the office, but he was quickly learning that he much preferred to see her like this, casual and sexy. As she made her way to him, he got an eyeful of her legs, remembering how they had felt wrapped around him the night before. He hoped that the talk they were about

to have would clear the way for that to happen again —
immediately.

"Hi Cole," Ember said as she slid in the booth. She immediately grabbed a menu, eager for something to do with her
hands.

"Good afternoon Ember. What do you think of this place?
It would make a great selling point in a print advertisement,
don't you think?" Cole said. His mind had drawn a blank when
he heard his name in her voice and he honestly didn't know
how to start the conversation they needed to have, so he was
stalling with small talk. Usually, he just laid it all out on the line
but for some reason, with Ember, he was having a hard time
finding a place to start.

"I think it would be perfect for print, but let's talk about
that later. I think we have something more important to talk
about right now, don't you think?" Ember looked up from her
menu and made direct eye contact with Cole. Her nerves
couldn't take business talk right now with all of this hanging
over their heads. She wanted to get their personal discussion
out of the way.

Cole was caught off guard by her blunt response but he recovered quickly. "You're right, we do. Last night was . . . so
damn good. That's the only way I can describe it. I'd like to
do it again, a lot, but I feel that we should be clear on what we
want from this," Cole said, taking the lead.

"I agree. I'm not interested in a relationship Cole. Not
now, probably not ever. My career is my focus and to be honest, I hold no illusions about marriage. I'm pretty sure I won't
get married. I agree that last night was damn good and I would
also like to do it again but there can be no illusions of a future
for us. As they say about Vegas, what happens on this ship
stays on this ship." Ember stared straight into Cole's eyes, driving home her point.

Well shit, Cole thought, *she said what I was going to say almost word for word.* "We are on the same page commitment-wise. Are you sure you want it to end with the cruise? We could continue on after we returned as long as we are discreet."

"No. We only know Warren here, but at home we know too many people and I work for you. The last thing I need in my career is to be categorized as the boss' concubine. It would be a complication I don't need nor do I want."

Cole nodded his head in agreement. Although he wouldn't mind continuing on after returning home, she was right. With her position in the company she had much more to lose. "I understand. We'll enjoy our time together and then that will be it. I do have one question."

Ember raised an eyebrow. "Sure."

"Are you on birth control?"

Cole watched as confusion and then realization hit her face.

"We didn't use protection last night," she said, stating the obvious.

"No, we didn't. I'm never, ever that careless. Now I understand the cliché of being swept away in the moment," Cole explained.

"I'm never careless about anything, much less something so important, so the cliché got me, too. I've been on birth control since I was 15 years old. I never miss a pill. I've never been pregnant, so they must work. I also have a clean bill of health, so you don't have to worry about that either."

"I have a clean bill as well, so we should be fine. I think we should use condoms going forward, though. Can't be too careful, right?" Cole said with a smile.

"Right," Ember agreed and then let an internal deep breath out. That was out of the way and they could move on to enjoying their time on the ship.

"So, you'll be my date for this trip?" Cole said, wiggling his eyebrows in a suggestive way, making Ember laugh out loud.

"Yes, I will be your date for the cruise." The tension of the talk was broken and they both felt at ease. Ember began to read the menu again. "This menu is full of authentic soda shop food. Awesome if you eat beef and pork. Not so awesome if you don't," she remarked as she scanned the many types of angus beef burgers and hot dogs with every topping imaginable.

"Not so fast. Flip the menu over," Cole instructed.

Ember did so and saw in big letters "No beef? No pork? No meat? No Problem!" Listed were turkey burgers, mushroom burgers, chicken hot dogs and an array of seafood and meatless options. A genuine smile lit up her face and she looked at Cole. "There's a whole side just for us!" Cole smiled back and ignored the way his skin came alive when she said us.

They studied the menu for a few more moments and then Cole signaled the waitress that they were ready to order. Once their orders were taken, they discussed ways to market the café, the dance deck, and the ballroom where they had eaten last night. About midway through their meal, as they were trying to decide whether they would check out the casino or the pool deck once they were finished, Ember looked up to see Vinny headed their way. She audibly groaned, stopping Cole mid-sentence. He looked up and saw Vinny as well, just as he was reaching their table. He groaned as well, though it sounded more like a growl.

"Hi Vinny, what can we do for you?" Cole said, making an attempt to sound friendly.

"Good afternoon Cole. Actually, I was coming over to see if Ember had any vacation behavior planned for this evening or if she was free for dinner."

"Vacation behavior?" Cole asked.

"Yes, you know, going with the flow and having a good time. It's how Ember told me she wants to spend her time on the ship," Vinny explained. Cole's eyebrow nearly reached his hairline as he digested Vinny's explanation.

"No, Vinny, I do not have any plans as of yet. Honestly, I may skip a formal dinner and spend my evening in the casino. I haven't made any plans and I don't intend to," Ember replied.

"Well, maybe I will see you in the casino later. I won a few hands last night and I'll see if I can win a few more tonight. How was your breakfast? It looked delicious. I caught a glimpse before I left this morning," Vinny asked.

Red hot rage washed over Ember because, although she knew what had really happened this morning, the way Vinny stated it seemed like they had spent the night together and he had left before she ate. *The fucking nerve of him!* She silently screamed in her head. Ember couldn't decide if she wanted to curse him out, punch him in the neck or both.

Cole observed the exchange with a closed mouth until this point, allowing Ember to handle her business but judging from the look on her face, things were about to get ugly. As much as he would love to see Ember, or anyone really, go off on Vinny he didn't want a scene as they were still here on business. He held his hand up, garnering both of their attention. "Ember has made it pretty clear that her vacation behavior includes no plans. If she sees you, she sees you. If she doesn't, take that as a hint. Now please leave us to finish our meal," he requested with an edge to his voice that indicated his anger was present but controlled . . . for now.

Vinny paused for a second and seemed to contemplate whether he wanted to challenge Cole's obvious dismissal. He decided to back down for now but not without a parting shot. "Of course. Enjoy your meal. I hope it's a working lunch; I happen to know your competition has some tricks up their sleeves. Enjoy." He didn't look back as he weaved his way out of the café.

"I know we should remain professional, but that dude almost caught these hands just now," Ember announced.

Hearing her speak like that caught Cole so off guard that he busted out laughing. Ember realized what she said and how she said it and soon joined in with Cole's laughter. The tense spell had been broken, but Ember wanted the air clear in case Cole was in any way feeding into the crap that Vinny had said.

"For the record, Vinny came knocking at my door this morning asking if I wanted to have breakfast with him. I told him I was not interested in making plans during my vacation, which I called vacation behavior. While he was standing in my doorway, not my cabin, room service arrived with my breakfast. He left before I even began eating," Ember explained.

"No need to explain. I read it for what it was: Vinny being a douchebag. Besides, you were knocked out when I left. No way you woke up from that until the morning," Cole laughed.

Ember blushed at both the implication and the memory. "Indeed," was her only reply.

"So, I know you don't want to make plans . . . "

"That was purely for Vinny's sake, we can make all the plans we want," Ember laughed.

"Well, then I propose we go to the pool for a few hours and then hit up the casino. Then we can see where the night leads us," Cole offered.

Ember's body warmed with the thought of where she wanted the night to lead. To be quite honest, she didn't want to wait for the night but she knew that they couldn't just lock themselves in a cabin and stay in bed the entire trip. They needed to experience all that Soul Escapes had to offer. "Sounds good to me. I just need to get changed," she replied.

"How about I pick you up at your place in about an hour and we walk up together?"

"Sounds like a plan," she laughed.

Chapter Sixteen

Ember looked at herself in the mirror and wondered what she was thinking when she let Cheyenne and Gabriella talk her into buying this swimsuit. They had insisted it looked amazing on her, and she agreed that she did look damn good, but now she thought maybe it was too much. The bikini was a retro style, with a halter-top and ties on each side of the bottom. The fabric was a deep gold hue with orange circles of varying sizes on it. Her matching sarong sported the same pattern, but the fabric was shear and her lower half could be seen clearly beneath it. Her hair was still up in a puff but she tied an orange scarf around it and tied the ends in a bow at the back of her puff. She looked like a sexy beach bunny from the 1960's.

She had two other bathing suits with her, one didn't cover much more than the bikini she was already wearing, but the other was a red one piece halter that was reminiscent of a 1950's pin up. She was about to change when she heard a knock at the door. Damn, had she used all her time being in-decisive? *Well, I can't just leave him out there knocking while I change, so I guess the bikini is it.* She thought to herself as she went to open the door.

The door swung open and Cole saw Ember standing there looking like an ebony beach goddess. The air left his body and desire quickly replaced it. His pupils dilated and his nose flared. He stepped inside, never taking his eyes off of her, and swung the door closed. He dropped his towel, wrapped his arms around her, and leaned in to capture her mouth. His hands roamed her body, touching as much uncovered skin as they could. Damn, it felt like she was made of satin. He slid his hand into her bikini bottom, grabbing the soft flesh housed there and caressing it. Ember let out a sigh on his lips and he pulled back to look in her eyes.

"You look good enough to eat," he announced as he began walking her backwards to the bed.

"Do I now?" she whispered.

"Yes, and I need a taste."

He gently pushed her down on the bed and she scooted back to make room for him to join her. But he motioned for her to stop. "I meant what I said, Ember," he reiterated, dropping to the side of the bed and pulling her back to the edge. He leaned in, placing his face between her legs and inhaling her scent. Ember now understood his intent and heat rushed through her body and settled at her core. Cole locked eyes with her has he reached to untie her sarong. It fell to the side, softly caressing her hips and thighs on the way down. He then slowly slid her bikini bottom down her legs, trailing his fingers behind them until it fell off her feet and onto the floor. Ember drew her legs up and opened them, giving Cole an unrestricted view of what he craved. He looked at her womanhood, feasting his eyes on what he had touched but never seen. She was perfect, neatly trimmed and he swore it was smiling at him, inviting him in. "Damn, you're beautiful," he breathed just as he leaned in.

The moment Cole's mouth touched her, Ember's body began to combust. She felt him place kisses all over her folds and then his tongue touched her clit and began to circle it with long, languid licks. Her hips started to buck up and down and he reached up to hold her steady as he latched on and began to suck and lick her in tandem. He created an erotic rhythm that danced touches of fire across her body and she began to come unhinged. She gripped his arms that were still holding her hips and dug her nails in, trying to fight off the orgasm she felt building; she didn't want this to end yet. Cole reveled in the feel of her nails in his arms, knowing it was an indication of her losing control. He continued his dance across her clit and she dug in harder and he could feel her hips trying to buck. After a few more seconds he felt her pulsate against his mouth and she screamed out her release. He looked up to watch her ride the waves of her orgasm and then come down from the high. Her breathing started to even out and she leaned up to look at him.

"I take it you like my bathing suit?" Ember whispered.

Cole picked up her bikini bottom and twirled it on one finger. "It's alright," he replied and then laughed at her raised eyebrow. "Okay, it's smoking hot. I'm glad I came to your room to get you instead of meeting you at the pool. I don't know if you can get arrested on a ship, but I'm sure there are still indecent behavior laws out at sea. Speaking of the pool, we still need to head on out. You need a moment to get . . . situated?"

Ember surprised that he wasn't looking for a return on the favor he had just given her. "We're leaving now?" she asked.

Cole read the question behind her question. "Yes but don't worry, you can pay me back later. And I got as much out of that as you did, believe me," he replied honestly.

Ember felt heat rush through her again. It was time to get up before she tried to convince him that the pool could wait until tomorrow. She grabbed her bikini bottom and excused herself to the bathroom. When she emerged, Cole was looking out of the porthole window. "It's crazy how we're in the middle of the ocean," she said, joining him at the window.

"Yeah, it is, but I kind of like it. I love what I do but it's all consuming and there's very little time to decompress."

"I know the feeling," Ember said with a chuckle.

In the back of Cole's mind, he knew she worked hard but it wasn't until now that he realized that many times she was one of the last people to leave the office. And he knew that she came in early a few times a week as well. Her efforts helped secure and keep many of their larger accounts. The bottom line was that Ember was invaluable to the firm. She deserved this vacation too. He wanted to thank her for her hard work, but he felt he could do better than words. He reached over and caressed her arm and then gave her a gentle tug toward him. Ember's heart began to pound and she went willingly into his arms. He leaned down to kiss her and she met him halfway. The moment their lips touched and electric current ran through both of them. The other kisses they shared were lustful and frantic, but this one was different. This kiss was slow and passionate and earth moving. Ember swayed slightly and Cole grasped her around the waist. They continued on for what felt like forever and no time at all, until they had to come up for air. Cole rested his forehead on hers. "If we keep this up, we'll never leave this room."

"And that's a bad thing, right?" Ember asked.

"No . . . well yes, because we need to experience the cruise. But no, because I have some things I want to experience with you," Cole answered honestly, regret in his voice.

"Like fantasies? Because I have fantasies too."

Heat rushed through Cole's body. Just hearing Ember say fantasy was a fantasy come true for him. "Yes, fantasies. You can tell me yours and I'll tell you mine . . . later, when we can put them into play." He took a deep breath and exhaled loudly. "Now let's get out of here before we get distracted again." Cole said as he walked to the cabin door.

"Yes, lets," Ember agreed. She grabbed the straw hat she had purchased from the ship's general store on the way back from lunch and then walked through the door Cole was holding open for her.

Chapter Seventeen

Ember had a hard time concentrating on enjoying the cool water in the pool. Her attention was on Cole, the way his red swim trunks rode low on his hips, and the muscular torso above them. He was the very definition of sexy. A chocolate Adonis. She felt like she could look at him forever, but she also knew her time to indulge was limited so she viewed her fill, often locking eyes with Cole as she caught him returning the looks she was giving him.

When they were in danger of turning into raisins, they decided to find a place to lounge and enjoy the scenery. They found an open cabana and Ember got comfortable while Cole got them drinks from the bar. She watched the people in the pool splashing and playing. The main pool was large and cascaded down into three smaller pools. There was a small lazy river and there were people floating around, drinking from coconuts, and sunning themselves. Cole reappeared with their drinks, a kamikaze for himself and a glass of moscato for Ember, and settled down next to her.

"This pool area is amazing," he remarked.

"I agree. I was just making mental notes about what should be included in our materials."

"Me too. I was also thinking that my sister would never leave this pool if she were here and neither would her friends. Just like I think the casino ads should target older adults, say forty and up, the pool may be best for late teens to mid-twenties. I see a lot of that age range out here. We should check the age and sex demographic and create specific materials aimed at them. Of course we would still do general ads, but it couldn't hurt to target some age ranges as well."

"I agree. You have a sister? I thought it was just you and your two brothers."

"Yes, we have a bratty little sister. Her name is Onyx and she's 23. She was a surprise and she's been a handful ever since. We tried to bargain to give her back, but my mom wasn't willing to give up the only other woman in a house full of men," Cole chuckled.

"So that's Cole, Rock, Micah and Onyx? Your parents don't like rocks and minerals, do they?"

"Dad is an amateur gemologist and geologist. He has books upon books on rock formations and precious stones. He named all of us. I assume mom was too exhausted to argue."

"I like it. You all are connected by more than just your last name and your names have meaning."

"That they do. What about you? Any siblings and are they named Fire and Gasoline?" Cole asked and they both laughed.

"Nope, it's just me. I'm the only child of only children. Both of my parents and all of my grandparents are dead. I'm the last in my line."

"Wow. You really are. Was it hard growing up an only child? I was almost two when Rock was born so I can't remember a time when I was by myself."

"It wasn't hard as much as it was lonely sometimes. But I did have Cheyenne. We grew up together. She's an only child too, although she has a whole slew of cousins. Then once we got to college we met Gabriella and Violet and I haven't had a lonely moment since," she said with a laugh.

"I bet you haven't. Your friends are very entertaining. I assume Violet is also a close friend of yours. Did something happen to her?" Ember's face dropped and sadness clouded her eyes. "You don't have to answer. I just remember Cheyenne saying there used to be four of you when we were having drinks the other day. I'm sorry if I upset you."

"No, it's okay. I have to get used to this." Ember took a deep breath. "It's a long story. Are you sure you want to hear it?" she asked.

"If you are willing to tell it, yes I'd like to hear it." Something compelled Cole to want to know what happened, even if it was just so he could figure out a way to help ease the pain he saw in her eyes.

"Violet disappeared about six months ago. She was dating a man for a while, but she was very secretive about him. All we really knew was his first name. The four of us were always so close; we never kept secrets from each other. Violet started distancing herself from us. No matter how hard we pushed, she wouldn't tell us anything besides his name and that she was happy. The more she distanced herself, the more worried we became. She kept telling us not to worry but in the last month before she disappeared I only saw her once or twice and we all hung out nearly every day, at the very least four to five times a week.

Cheyenne had a really hard time with it because she and Violet were roommates. She tried to get Violet to tell her why she was so distant but Violet would not budge. One day Violet came home distraught. Cheyenne took one look at her and immediately called me and Gab. It took us over an hour to get her calm and then all she did was clam up and refuse to talk about what ever upset her. After she went to sleep that night, the three of us talked and decided to take her on a girls' trip that weekend. When Cheyenne woke up the next morning,

Violet was gone. We called her multiple times. Her phone kept going to voice mail. We waited for her all night Friday night.

When we still hadn't heard from her by Sunday afternoon, I wanted to call the police but Cheyenne is weary of the police and wanted to see if we could find her on our own. We went into her room to see if she left any hint of where she went. What we found was her phone, which had been powered off, her purse with her wallet in it, and every stitch of clothing she owned in her closet except for the clothes she had been wearing the last time we saw her. That was when we knew we had to call the police. They could not find a trace of her.

We hired a private detective who searched for months. He found nothing. It's like she just disappeared. And neither the police nor the private investigator found the guy she was seeing. I guess with only a first name, it's hard to track someone down. Cheyenne is convinced that things went bad between Violet and the mystery guy and she killed herself. Gabriella is on the fence but after six months with no trace, she's starting to believe that Violet may have actually committed suicide. I don't believe that shit for one second. Violet was one of the strongest people I know. She would never kill herself and certainly not over a man. She went through a bad break up with her ex fiancé and refused to let it get her down. And she was with that guy for years. I refuse to believe that she got through that but killed herself over a man that she didn't even know for a year."

"Don't get defensive, but let me ask you something."

"I won't . . ."

"Are you positive that Violet is still alive or are you leaning on the hope that she is still alive because you don't want to let her go?" Cole hoped he wasn't overstepping but he honestly wanted to know the answer.

"That's actually a question I've asked myself more than once in the last few months." Tears pooled in Ember's eyes. "I truly and honestly believe Violet is still alive, somewhere. I actually wish I could just let this go and bury her so to speak. It's hard knowing she's out there, hurting and possibly in trouble, and not being able to help her. I don't have biological family anymore. Violet, Cheyenne, and Gabriella are my only family. It's the equivalent of you having one of your siblings missing and not being able to do anything about it. Wouldn't it eat away at you?" she asked as tears began to slip from her eyes.

"No doubt. I'm sorry I upset you," he said as he reached out to wipe her tears away. "We don't have to talk about this anymore if you don't want to."

"Actually, it feels good to talk about it," she said as she got her tears in check. "My circle is small enough for target practice but strong enough to handle the bullets. It is pretty much composed of Cheyenne, Gabriella and Violet. I can't talk to Violet for obvious reasons. It's impossible to get Cheyenne to even see the possibility of what I'm saying. We always end up in shouting matches. That only leaves Gabriella, who I'm sure is tired of hearing me say Violet is alive while she's trying to figure out how she can process this. It's nice to be able to talk about it. Maybe nice isn't the right word. Refreshing? Relieving? Whatever."

Cole chuckled at her use of whatever. "I get it. So, what is your next step?"

"Honestly, I don't know. This is probably a cold case for the police now, especially with no new leads. I could try hiring a new PI, but the one we hired before came highly recommended. If he hit nothing but dead ends, I'm not sure what hiring another will do. Violet's only living relative is her grandmother and she gave Violet up for dead months ago. I'm stuck knowing she's out there but I have no way to find her and no support to do so anyway."

"That's definitely a rock and a hard place situation. I'm always here to talk. Like you said, just talking will help you feel a little better. You have my ear," Cole said earnestly. He felt a strong sense of needing to be there for her, to help her through this.

"I truly appreciate that," she closed her hand over his. The gesture was supposed to be one of appreciation but the moment her hand touched his heat shot through her body and she locked eyes with him. He felt it too because his eyes darkened with desire and he leaned over and kissed her. It was their first public kiss, certainly more chaste than their others, but it held a promise of things to come and Ember found herself looking forward to alone time later on.

When the kiss ended, Cole pulled away and gave himself a mental shake. He couldn't put his finger on it but something was different about this kiss. He didn't want to read into it, so instead he checked the time.

"We've been out here for quite a while. You want to go get changed and head out to the casino? We could grab something to eat at the buffet and then try not to lose our shirts at the blackjack table," he proposed.

"I don't do blackjack but I love slot machines."

"Why don't we meet around six? That's almost two hours to relax and get dressed. Honestly I might get in a quick power nap."

"Six it is and I might get a power nap in myself. Who knows how long we'll be in the casino. If I win, I'll stay there all night," she laughed.

"You and me both. Let's head out then."

They were unaware of the two sets of eyes watching them, as they gathered themselves and headed to their rooms. The eyes, however, were very aware of them.

Chapter Eighteen

"Why are you calling me from a cruise? You have to have better things to do than to burn up my line," Rock asked.

"Damn, I don't even get a hello? Indeed I do have better things to do, but I need a favor," Cole said with a chuckle.

"Hi Cole. Now, why are you calling me from a cruise?" Rock asked again.

"I need a favor, super sleuth."

"You mean: I need a favor best PI in the world," Rock countered.

"I mean: I'll kick your ass if you don't help me," Cole warned.

"The day I worry about an ass whupping from you is the day . . . I can't think of such a day ever existing. What do you want?"

"I need you to look into the disappearance of one of Ember's friends. A woman named Violet. She's been missing roughly six months."

"She's been missing six months? Were the police involved?"

"Yes, nothing but dead ends. Ember even hired a PI. She claimed he came highly recommended but I'm pretty sure I know a better one," Cole joked.

"Pretty sure? More like damn certain. And leaning on my superlative PI skills, I feel the need to ask why you are interested in this case."

"Ember told me the story today and she seems adamant that Violet wouldn't kill herself. The story she told me makes me lean toward agreeing with her."

"So you and Ember have been spending a lot of time together then?" Rock asked.

"Mind your business," Cole warned.

"You are my business. Especially since you dragged me into this last week or did you forget the poker game?"

Cole sighed with annoyance, but Rock was right. "Yes, we've been spending time together."

"Time or *time*?"

"What difference does it make? Time is time. Are you going to help or not?" Agitation was evident in Cole's voice.

"Yeah it's *time* or you wouldn't be so defensive. And you want to help her so you're in your feelings about her too," Rock concluded.

"Dammit, it's not like that. Are you going to help or not? I'm only asking this one last time," Cole warned.

"Get a grip, Cole. Of course I'll help. Let me grab something to write with . . . okay, what's Violet's last name?"

"I don't know."

"Last known address?"

"She and Cheyenne were roommates."

"What the hell does that mean? I need you to give me something to go on here. Just ask Ember and then get back to me."

"I can't ask Ember. She doesn't know I'm enlisting your help and I don't want her to unless you come back with proof that Violet is still alive. I don't want to get her hopes up," Cole explained.

"Don't want to get her hopes up . . . hmmmmmm . . ."

"What the hell are you hmmmmming about?" Cole demanded.

"You have feelings for Ember," Rock stated bluntly.

"You don't know what you're talking about. I just want to help her out."

"Because you have feelings for her . . ." Rock reiterated.

"I have feelings for no woman. Are you going to help or not? I have somewhere to be in twenty minutes" Cole decided to leave out that the somewhere was in the casino with Ember.

"Okay okay. I need to get all of the information you can give me. Start from the beginning and tell me everything Ember told you," Rock requested.

Fifteen minutes later, Cole hung up with Rock and sat at the table, thinking about what Rock had said. Did he have feelings for Ember? He was feeling more than just a physical attraction to her that was for sure. But what was he going to do about it? They had mutually agreed that their time together was limited to the cruise. Could he convince her to continue on after they returned home? Is that what he wanted? He looked at his watch and realized he was supposed to be meeting Ember at that moment. He didn't have the time to figure it out right now. It would have to wait until later.

* * *

Ember watched Cole walk toward her and decided that he looked good in a pair of jeans. Very good. She watched his jungle cat swagger and remembered how his powerful thighs had held her up against the door in her room as he pumped in and out of her the night before. Had that only been 24 hours ago? It seemed like much longer and yet looking ahead it seemed like their time together was growing shorter and shorter. She would be disappointed when the cruise was over but things were the way they were and nothing would change that. At least she would have the memories.

"Hey. Sorry I'm late. I had to make a phone call and it ran a bit longer than I thought," Cole explained.

"No problem. You're only a few minutes late. Everything okay?" Ember asked.

"Yup. Everything is all good. Including that dress. I'm glad we met up here instead of me coming to your room first. We would likely not have ever made it up here," he said eying the short, black sundress Ember was wearing appreciatively.

"I'm glad you like it," Ember said with a wink and then turned around to head into the casino.

Cole watched the seductive sway of her hips for a few seconds before following. "What do you want to do first?" he asked.

"I know you said you like to play blackjack. I don't really like that too much. I prefer slot machines but I wouldn't mind roulette if you want to play a table game together," she offered.

"Nope, I'm good with slot machines. If you want to pick two machines together, I'll go get us some change," Cole said.

"Sounds good." She dug in her wristlet and pulled out 2 one hundred dollar bills and handed to him. "Quarters please. The penny, nickel, and dime machines will just nickel and dime you." She walked away laughing at her own joke.

Cole had not expected Ember to give him money and he smiled at the fact that she had. He was used to women expecting him to pay for everything and he usually did because, well, he could. But Ember hadn't seemed to even contemplate it. Cole marveled at how refreshing that was as he walked over to get her coins and two hundred dollars worth for him as well and then wove his way around the maze of slot machines to find Ember. Just as he was sitting down at the machine to her left, Vinny came walking by. Ember prepared herself to send him packing but he simply nodded in their direction and continued on his way. His demeanor was indifferent, but his eyes were angry.

"Well, someone is salty," Ember observed as she added her first coin to the slot machine and pulled the lever.

"I'm just glad he kept on walking," Cole said, mirroring her actions. The two sat and played and talked for the next hour or so. They bounced around ideas for highlighting the casino in ads and discussed the finer art of gambling. Cole got up to get drinks and he arrived back just in time to see Ember's machine start ringing and flashing lights. The big $2,500 neon sign over the machine blinked on and off and a horn seemed to blow out of nowhere. She jumped up and started dancing around and clapping her hands. Cole sat the drinks down at a nearby table and stood to watch her. She was definitely something to behold. He joined her in her celebration and they did a quick salsa dance before a casino official walked up to disengage the machine and award Ember her winning voucher.

Cole and Ember laughed as they sat back down in front of their machines to recover from the excitement.

"Well, I was not expecting that. I never win anything," Ember remarked.

"It was a hell of a win. You were only about half way through your bucket of quarters, so that was a $100 investment that yielded a $2,400 net profit. The odds were definitely in your favor," Cole calculated.

"Definitely!" Ember laughed.

"So, do you want to see if your luck will hold out on this machine or do you want to try another one?" Cole asked.

Ember looked him square in the eyes and replied, "I'd rather go back to your room and celebrate."

Chapter Nineteen

Heat shot through Cole's body as he decided that Ember's mouth had the potential to be his undoing if she ever decided to use it against him. He grabbed his coin bucket and held out his hand, indicating he wanted Ember to join him.

"Hey, we have to cash our coins and my voucher in first!" Ember laughed.

The look on Cole's face was a clear indication of his impatience. He spent the longest ten minutes of his life cashing out their money and then he and Ember hurried through the door, down the hall to the elevator, and arrived at his door in record time. Cole unlocked the door and pulled Ember through. She sat her things down on the table and turned to face him just as he put the do not disturb sign on the door and then Cole closed the distance between them. He whispered, "This time we'll make it to the bed, I promise," and then captured her mouth in a hungry kiss.

Ember's body was on fire. She raised her arms to circle his neck and returned Cole's kiss, savoring his taste and again deciding he was her favorite flavor. She felt his strong arms wrap around her waist and then move down to pull her dress up her legs. When it was bunched at her waist, he slid his hands into her panties, caressing her backside skin to skin. He turned her around and again wrapped his arms around her middle, this time resting his hands over her mound and lightly caressing it. Ember felt liquid heat pool between her legs and she pushed her hips out, begging Cole to touch her where she needed it the most. He answered her request by sliding his hand into her panties and slipping his middle finger between the lips of her sex to rub her clit. She exhaled, not realizing that she had been holding her breath and began to grind against his finger. She could feel his hardness behind her and it fueled her fire as the waves of a powerful orgasm took control of her. Cole clasped her tighter as she pulsed against his hand. He held her until she had recovered enough to walk to the bed, as he still held her from behind. He turned her once more then reached down to grasp the bottom of her dress and pull it over her head.

Ember stood before him in a pair of lace boy shorts and a matching black lace bra. She was beautiful but he needed to see more. He removed her sandals and reached for her bra to do the same. He stared at her flawless breasts, the dark nipples stood at attention. Cole cupped them, rubbing his thumbs across their sensitive peaks, and listened to Ember sigh her pleasure. He tore his attention away to focus on the last piece of clothing she wore, her panties. He slid them down her legs and she kicked them away. Cole stood and looked at the woman in front of him. She was an ebony goddess, full of beauty and grace and he wanted nothing more than to be buried inside of her. He quickly removed his clothing.

Ember didn't demurely look away as most women he had encountered would have. She openly stared at his nakedness, drinking him in and smiling with appreciation. This enticed him even more and he quickly laid her on the bed and joined her, positioning himself between her legs as she bent her knees and drew her legs back, giving him full view of her womanhood. He splayed his hands across her abdomen and caressed her stomach and thighs, then briefly dipped his finger inside of her to make sure she was wet and ready. She was and he positioned himself to enter her. He sealed their bodies together and her body fit him like a glove. He was buried to the hilt when he realized that once again they had failed to use protection. He froze and looked at her, not wanting to disengage their bodies but knowing it was her call. Her response was to lift her hips and begin grinding against him. It was all the answer he needed.

He grasped her hips and began to slide in and out of her. They created their own rhythm, the melody of their joined bodies swirling around, encasing them until it became fever pitch and Ember came apart screaming Cole's name. As she came down from her high, Cole turned her around so that she was on all fours in front of him. As he entered her from behind, she felt him stretch her in new ways and touch new places. He began to move in and out and soon Ember was rearing back and meeting him, thrust for thrust. The sounds of their bodies meeting vibed with the sighs of pleasure Ember was releasing. They moved faster and faster until she felt him tense and groan out his release just before she tumbled over the edge again. He pulsed inside of her as her own orgasm milked his body of all he had to give. She collapsed onto the bed as Cole rolled over onto his back. She had done doggy style before but it had never felt like it did with Cole. Sex had never felt like it did with Cole. Once her breathing returned back to normal she rolled over to face him and he rolled from his back to meet her half way.

"Tired?" he asked.

"Absolutely."

"Sleep?"

"For now," she replied.

He chuckled as he covered them. "Insatiable woman."

"You like it," Ember replied, stifling a yawn.

As he drifted to sleep Cole decided that he did indeed like it.

Chapter Twenty

Ember woke up to the feeling of her backside cradled against Cole's groin, his masculine arm thrown across her torso, and his hand cupping her breast. She had never awakened like this before but she could see why women liked to be spooned. It felt like she belonged to Cole and she decided that she liked that feeling, however temporary it may be. She listened to his even breathing and wondered how, in less than a week, he had somehow gone from her being her standoffish boss to the man she couldn't get enough of.

She would never admit it out loud but she wished things were different so she and Cole could continue their affair after they returned home. Her body craved him. Even now, just thinking about him had moisture pooling between her legs. She used to wonder how women got so caught up in a man. She would watch her female classmates chase after men and go through all kinds of changes. It's still not something Ember thought she would do but now she saw how that could easily happen. It would be hard to let Cole go in a few days, but it was what she had to do.

Ember felt Cole grow hard behind her and the hand cupping her breast began to massage her nipple. He was awake.

"Good morning," Cole whispered in her ear.

"Good morning yourself," she replied. Cole continued to strum her nipple and she chuckled. "I know where this is going. I know morning sex is supposed to be amazing but I'm not a fan. All I can think of is how sweaty and . . . uh . . . juicy we got last night. I think I'm going to hit the shower," Ember explained, hoping it wouldn't upset him.

"A woman after my own heart," he replied, although he did not cease his attention to her nipple. Instead, he rolled her over and gave each nipple a quick kiss before releasing her so she could head to the bathroom.

Just before she cleared the bathroom door, she looked back at him and said, "But, feel free to join me," and then disappeared from sight.

Cole rolled over onto his back and put his arms behind his head. He had every intention on taking her up on her offer but first he wanted to take a moment to exhale. He had watched Waiting to Exhale years ago with his sister and never quite understood it, so he assumed it was a woman thing. But now he got it. It was the ability to exhale because everything had come together and everything was right. It wasn't a woman thing; it was a fulfilled thing. These last few days with Ember had been the best days he'd had in as long as he could remember. He was never this happy with Denise or any of the women after her. This was solely because of Ember. He knew he was being selfish but he didn't want their time to end when got home. There had to be a way to continue the affair without compromising her position with the company. Cole got up and headed to the bathroom, deciding he would think about that later. Right now Ember was in the shower waiting for him.

Through the glass shower door he could see Ember standing under the showerhead. The water was cascading down her body and she looked like a water goddess. His body immediately reacted to the sight and he quickly undressed then stepped in the shower. Ember stepped back to give Cole access to the spray. He tilted his head back and wet his face. He caught a bit of water in his mouth and swished it around, spit it out, and then smiled at Ember.

"Quick dose of morning breath be gone," he explained.

"I did the same thing," she chuckled. "You use the same soap I do," she said, indicating the bar of African black soap sitting in the soap holder.

"Well isn't that lucky for us?" Cole replied as he picked up the soap and began to create a lather in his hands. He sat the bar down and began to soap Ember's upper body, starting at her shoulders and slowly making his way down to her breasts. He made sure to pay special attention to her nipples. Ember sighed and enjoyed his touch. There was something almost magical about the way the steam from the shower swirled around them as he explored her body. Cole grabbed the soap again but Ember took it from him.

"You don't think you get to have all the fun, do you?" she asked as she created her own lather and then ran her hands through the hair on his chest. The hair acted as a catalyst and created even more suds, which she spread all over him from his neck to the bottom of his torso. He groaned as her hands moved lower, grasping his manhood. She grabbed the soap again and came back to soap his lower half. As she grasped his shaft, Cole was in both heaven and hell. Her touch was heavenly, but he wanted like hell to be inside of her. Ember continued down his body and soaped his strong thighs. Cole felt like he was about to bust wide open.

He needed to get control of the situation or he wasn't going to make it out alive. He put his arms around Ember's waist and pulled her close, connecting their soapy bodies and, then he turned her around. He grabbed the soap once more and returned to her back with fresh suds. He worked to soap down her back and across her backside and then surprised her by reaching around her, caressing her hips and then moving lower. He soaped the front of her thighs and then reached between her legs. Ember pushed back and grinded against him.

"Why don't we rinse off and take this back into the bed," Cole suggested.

"Absolutely."

When they reached the bed, Ember pushed Cole down and climbed on top of him. She leaned over and gave him a searing kiss, letting her nipples lightly graze his chest. Cole brought his hands up and rubbed her hips and backside. Moisture once again pooled between her legs. She positioned herself over his manhood and slowly slid down. She marveled at how perfectly they fit together just before she began to slowly ride. Cole was caught in ecstasy as she moved. He grasped her hips and began to meet her thrust for thrust. Each time she came down, he buried himself to the hilt. He watched as her breasts bounced up and down, their buds so tight they looked like brown pearls. Ember rode him harder and he knew he wasn't going to make it much longer. He reached forward and rubbed his thumb over her clit. Seconds later she tumbled over the edge into a leg-shaking, soul clenching orgasm. Cole followed seconds later and Ember reveled in the feeling of him pulsing inside of her. She collapsed on his chest and he wrapped his arms around her. They stayed like that for a while.

Then Ember's stomach growled. Cole chuckled. "I guess we better feed you, huh?"

"I am starving. You have to be hungry too."

"Oh, no doubt. Let's figure out what to order."

Forty-five minutes later Cole and Ember were sitting at the table in his room eating waffles and trying to figure out what to do with their day. Cole was bare chested and wearing a pair of boxer briefs. As hungry as Ember was, she was having a hard time concentrating on eating when Cole looked good enough to eat himself. Likewise, Cole appreciated how good Ember looked wrapped in the robe from his bathroom. Liquid anger briefly shot through him when he realized that Vinny had seen Ember dressed exactly like this the morning before. He had a strong desire to knock the man's teeth out for seeing his woman that way.

His woman.

Where the hell had that come from? He wondered. *Is that what Ember was?* Cole was beginning to think she might just be. The only problem was that she didn't want to be. You can't be in a relationship with someone who is unwilling to be there. Did he want a relationship? Ember waved her hands in front of his face and he realized he had zoned out in his thoughts.

"Are you there Cole?" Ember asked.

"Hmmm? Yes. What were you saying?"

"You do that a lot, huh?"

"Do what?" he asked.

"Get lost in your thoughts."

"Not until recently," he admitted. *And only when I think of you,* he thought to himself.

"Uh huh. Well, I was saying that we are supposed to be docked in Nassau from 8am until 5pm today. It's 11:15 and I don't feel the ship moving so I assume we have docked. Are we going to make it out of this room today so we can explore Nassau? I read about the Straw Market and I would love to visit it."

"As much as I would love to spend the rest of the day in the bed with you, we should go out into Nassau and check things out. Maybe some things in town will make for good additions to our pitch. The Straw Market sounds promising. What exactly is it?"

"According to the cruise information packet we got, it's an open market with handmade crafts and souvenirs. There are bags, dolls, hats, jewelry, hand carved wood art, and clothes. And all prices are not final. I love to haggle so they had me at "prices are negotiable,"" Ember said with a laugh.

"Yeah, that sounds like something we should definitely check out. We're just about done here. How long do you think you'll need to get back to your room and get ready?" Cole asked.

"I can be ready by 12:15. You want to come get me from my room or do you want me to meet you up at the dock?"

Cole remembered what happened the last time he met her at her room and smiled. "If we want to actually make it off the ship, we may want to play it safe and meet up at the dock. We need to check out Nassau and I can't be trusted to stay on the outside of your door once you open it."

Ember returned his smile and stood to put her dress from the night before back on. "So, 12:15 at the dock then?" she asked as she let the robe slip to the floor and stood naked in front of Cole for a split second before reaching for her dress and tugging it over her head.

Cole took a deep breath. "Yes and that's exactly why."

Ember laughed as she gathered her bra and purse and headed for the door.

"I'll see you in a little while," she called over her shoulder as she moved through the door. Cole was slightly disappointed that she hadn't given him a kiss goodbye. He walked toward the bathroom to take a second shower and saw that Ember left her panties in the middle of the bed. He knew there was no way that was an oversight on her part; she had left them on purpose. *Now that's almost as good as a kiss* Cole thought as he walked into the bathroom.

Chapter Twenty-One

Cole watched Ember negotiate with a basket weaver and decided that not only did she clearly enjoy haggling, she was pretty damned good at it too. He might need to include her in the financial part of securing clients for Commercial Innovations in the future. He thought back to the first night they were on the boat when Vinny the Dick, as Cole had named him, said that Ember was the full package. At the time, Cole only knew she was smart and liked sports and he assumed that she could cook and balance a budget. In just two days he had learned she was so much more. He still thought she was smart but he also knew that she didn't look down her nose or act superior to others because of her intelligence. Her taste in sports teams was questionable but she did at least follow the Panthers. When they were at the casino they had talked about her love of baking and her ironic dislike of cooking. She'd won $2,500 last night but was still haggling with a street vendor today, so he was right about her being fiscally responsible. He'd learned that, though her circle of friends was small, she was fiercely loyal and protective of those she loved. And dammit was she sexy and amazing in bed. If he didn't already know, he would sincerely wonder why she wasn't some lucky man's pride and joy.

But he did know. She didn't want to be some lucky man's pride and joy. She made that abundantly clear. Too bad his heart wasn't listening. There was no way things could go back to normal after they got home. Absolutely no way. He would take one look at her and remember the sound of her laughter or the way she bucked her hips when he was plunging into her.

Ember left the booth and walked over to him. He could tell she had been victorious in her haggling. She was smiling ear to ear.

"Not only did I get him to knock $15 off of the price but I also talked him into weaving names into all of the straw baskets I bought. One for Cheyenne, Gabriella, Violet, and me." Ember paused for a second. "Is it crazy that I got one for Violet too?" she asked.

"No," he replied honestly. "You truly believe she is still alive."

"What about you?" she asked as they began to walk around the rest of the straw market. "You know the whole story. Do you think she's still alive?"

Cole stopped in front of a booth with woodcarvings and turned to look Ember in the eyes. "If this were Rock, Micah, or Onyx I would need to see a body before I let them go. I know that probably sounds morbid but I would. I don't care if there was a plane crash and officials claimed there were no survivors. I would have to hire someone to drag the woods or ocean or where ever the plane crashed and find me something that proved death before I would accept it. I would go to my grave looking for them. I would leave it in my will that someone continue trying to find out what happened. They would have to meet me on the other side and then I would be satisfied. Do you understand what I'm saying?"

"Yes and I appreciate that you don't think I'm crazy. I was beginning to wonder if I was."

Cole put his arm around her and pulled her close. "You are more than welcome. Now, oh haggling guru, help me pick out one of these carvings for my parents and haggle down the price. I defer to your infinite wisdom." He bowed in front of her and she threw her head back and laughed.

* * *

Ember sat in her room and looked at all the gifts she had purchased in Nassau. It was quite a bit but she had haggled great prices for them and she was more than satisfied with her purchases. She even purchased herself a beautiful necklace. The chain and pendant were white gold. The pendant had several brown and gold amber stones arranged in a circular pattern. She had always loved amber, partially because of how close it was to her name and partially because of how diverse amber stones could be. She had eyed the matching ring, which also had diamonds in it, but it was more than she was willing to spend.

It had been hot in Nassau. Very, very hot. Ember supposed that was what you got when you went on a Caribbean cruise in the middle of the summer. The heat had been downright disrespectful and invaded her personal space. Cole noticed her dragging and sent her back to the ship while he found a gift for his sister. She heard her phone alert that a text message had come through. Thank goodness her company allowed her the ability to pay a nominal fee instead of paying roaming fees in international waters. She picked up the phone and opened up her messages. She saw she had three. One was from Cheyenne.

"All this silence from you makes me think you have FINALLY got some sense. If I don't hear back from you I will assume that you have either decided to get with Sexy Cole or you have found a rich Caribbean man and become part of his harem. Do Caribbean men have harems?" Ember rolled her eyes at Cheyenne's perpetual insanity.

The second text was from Gabriella.

"That fool just showed me the text she sent you. It's been an hour and we haven't heard back so we're just going to assume you are . . . otherwise occupied. Enjoy!" She smiled, thinking that it was just like Gabriella to wish her good sex. Gab was a firecracker if you made her angry but generally she was a sweetheart.

Ember decided to let them wonder what she was up to. The third text was from Cole.

"I made it back on the ship just before they closed the port. They definitely don't run on CP time around here. I'm going to see Warren for a while. Text you when we're done," Ember responded with a simple, "Okay, have fun."

Although she knew that their time together was limited, she was getting a bit overwhelmed with her feelings and a break might be what she needed to get herself together. Today when she asked Cole if he thought Violet was still alive and he'd given her the answer, she almost melted right there and the oppressive heat had nothing to do with it. That answer was everything. Every. Single. Thing. Her mind kept floating to the thought that if things were different, if he wasn't her boss, if she believed in love, maybe he would be the one. But that line of thought was foolish at best and dangerous at worst. She would use this evening to veg out, decompress, and watch some TV. Not exactly what one typically did on a cruise ship but it sounded like heaven to her. First she would take a shower, then order a bunch of sinfully delicious room service, and then find a good movie. Then, later when Cole called, she would be ready.

Chapter Twenty-Two

"Well, you've created quite a shit storm for yourself haven't you, Scotch Bonnet?" Warren assessed as he swirled his whiskey around the ice in his glass. Cole rolled his eyes at the nickname he received while on line to join their fraternity. Warren was Jamaican and Cole's hot temper prompted him to name him after the popular Caribbean chili pepper.

"You know it wasn't my intent for this to happen. This is the exact opposite of how I thought this would turn out," Cole argued.

"Look, I like Ember. She's smart, gorgeous, and all of that. But this is exactly why you don't sleep with your employees. There's not a woman on this ship or at our corporate office that I would touch with a ten-foot pole. It's just bad business, you know?"

"On paper it is. But we have an understanding. And she was more than willing to keep it short and sweet. Hell, I proposed that we still see each other after the cruise was over and *she* said no. It was a failsafe plan," Cole explained and then took a sip from his glass.

"Except that apparently your heart wasn't informed of the plan."

"Fucking traitor," Cole mumbled.

"Indeed. I knew you were gone when I saw you two kissing at the pool yesterday. But I peeped you even before that. I watched you two the first night when we had dinner. You were clearly distracted by her. Someone who doesn't know you may have believed that bull about thinking about work but I know better. You had it bad then. You're just realizing it now. Yuh seen? " Warren clarified, making his point in patois.

"Why didn't you warn me if you saw all of this, then?" Cole demanded. "Never mind. We both know I wouldn't have listened. Matter of fact, I would've told you that you were crazy as hell and told you go somewhere with that shit," he admitted.

"Truth. Now what are you going to do? You went and fell in love with a woman who wants no part of love. That's a hell of a conundrum my friend."

"No idea. On one hand, I want to come clean and tell her how I feel. But that would most likely backfire and these last few days I have with her would be ruined. The bigger picture would be that I would have to work with a woman who knows I love her but doesn't love me back. That would be more painful that keeping it to myself."

"I can't imagine either one of you would last very long in an environment like that. And I'll admit this is purely selfish but I want you and Ember on my account. Your other ad-execs were good but Ember was the best and you two are the best I've ever seen. That is, of course, if Soul Escapes decides to hire you. If you ask me nicely, I might tell you if you won the account or not," Warren teased.

"I'm not taking that bait Warren. I know full well that you and Joseph haven't talked about a thing and you wouldn't make that decision on your own. Plus, if you had already decided on us, Vinny the Dick and his cousin wouldn't be here."

"Vinny the Dick?" Warren threw his head back in laugher. "Quite fitting, although he is a great ad-man. And you're right.

Joseph and I haven't discussed it and I wouldn't tell you anyway. His brother had some kind of medical crisis and I haven't spoken to him since he called to say he wouldn't make the cruise. He's very closed mouthed when it comes to family business so I'm not sure what's going on."

"Well, I do hope everything is okay," Cole said honestly. "Now back to me," he requested. "I should just keep all this to myself, right? She's made it crystal clear where she stands. Telling her anything would just complicate it and ruin the rest of our time here, right?"

"If it was me, that's what I would do. Then again, if it was me, I wouldn't be caught up in this mess," Warren said confidently.

"That's because you're a damn hermit hiding away on a cruise ship," Cole countered.

"And it's working out just fine for me. Being a hermit means no drama. I'm good," Warren concluded.

"One day you'll have to come ashore and deal with us land lubbers, you know."

"Not if I have anything to say about it. I'll happily live out my days on this ship and when I die, just throw me overboard. I'll be fine."

"Well, that's uncomfortable," Cole stated. He and Warren visited for a while longer, discussing sports and a little frat business. They were discussing the upcoming homecoming season when there was a knock on Warren's door. Warren got up to answer and Cole heard a familiar voice carry through the room.

"Good evening Warren. I know we are supposed to be enjoying all the ship has to offer, and believe me we are, but I wanted to see if you had time now or before we dock to talk about some ideas we have."

Warren pulled the door the rest of the way open. "Come in Vinny." Vinny strode in; his confidant steps faltered when he saw Cole sitting in his chair, nursing his glass of whiskey, and looking completely relaxed.

Serves his annoying ass right, Cole thought to himself. Aloud he said, "Good evening Vinny," with a smile that looked about as fake as a six-dollar bill.

"Good evening to you, Cole. If I'm interrupting something, I can come back."

"No need," Cole responded. "I was just getting ready to head out. I need to get some rest so I can be up early. We dock at Grand Turk at 7:30 and I'd like to get out early, before the temperature reaches full blown hell."

Warren chuckled. "The heat is an acquired taste but you get used to it after a while."

"Nope, I'm good." Cole said rising from his chair and heading to the door. "The black movie marathon is tomorrow, correct Warren?"

"Yes, 5-11pm in the movie theater. Seats are limited so I would go ahead and reserve yours now."

"Will do. You fellas have a great night," Cole called over his shoulder as he strode through the door. As he walked down the hallway he pulled out his phone and sent Ember a text.

"Are you still up? Just left Warren's suite. A dick crashed our party," he chuckled at his jab at Vinny and headed up to the ship's general store. He knew he could reserve his and Ember's seats for the movie night there and he was a little hungry and could grab a snack. His phone buzzed in his hand.

"Wide awake and about to watch Harlem Nights. We can sleep at my place tonight, lol. Bring snacks. Lots of snacks. Chocolate preferred. See you in a few."

Cole smiled as he typed his response. "Gonna pack an overnight bag, reserve our seats for the movie marathon tomorrow, and then get snacks. Don't start the movie without me. See you in a few."

Cole couldn't wait to get to her. He knew that he was right to not tell Ember how he felt. It sucked for him but it was the right thing for her. He had already lost his heart; if he told her how he felt he was sure that he would lose her as well. Better to love from afar and at least get to see her than to have her walk out of his life. That's all he had for now and he was going to hold on to it.

Chapter Twenty-Three

"A dick crashed your party, huh?" Ember inquired when she let Cole in her room twenty-five minutes later.

"You caught that, huh?" he asked as he sat his overnight bag on the floor and his bag of snacks on the table.

"Yup and I need details because that sounds like some kind of guy code has been broken," Ember said as she dug around in the snack bag and retrieved the first chocolate thing she could find. Cole watched her walk back over to her bed. She was wearing black leggings and an oversized college tee shirt. Her hair was still in the puff she had been wearing earlier but it must have loosened because there were stray curls making an escape. She looked sexy in a comfortable way and Cole was man enough to admit that he wouldn't mind coming home to see her dressed like this.

"Well, Warren and I were sitting around talking sports and homecoming activities when there was a knock on the door." Cole grabbed the snack bag off the table and joined her on the bed. When he had returned to his room to grab his clothes for tomorrow, he had also changed into sweat pants and a tee shirt because he figured they were going to lounge and watch Harlem Nights.

"And . . ."

"And it was Vinny the Dick."

"Seriously?"

"Yup. He wanted to have some one on one time with Warren to discuss some ad ideas. Little does he know it doesn't matter because Warren will not make a decision without Joseph and that means our boy Vinny will have to re-propose all of his ideas when Joseph is available again. I hope he didn't take up too much of Warren's time."

"He is so damn aggressive. It's almost like he has a Napoleon complex, but he's not short," Ember remarked.

"Yeah, that's just called being an asshole. He's an asshole."

Ember laughed as she pulled up the movie search box on the TV and began to type in Harlem Nights. "I don't know how they made it happen but Soul Escapes had every black movie ever made right here at your fingertips. It's amazing. I even found Sparkle. Be glad I had already committed to Harlem Nights before I found it because Sparkle is hands down my favorite movie. Ever."

"I've never seen Sparkle. Is that the Whitney Houston movie. Came out right before she died, right?"

"Blasphemy! I love Whitney and all but no. That was the remake. The original came out in late 1976 but the movie actually takes place in the late 50's. It has Irene Cara and Phillip Michael Thomas in it. It's about the music scene back then and how drugs corrupted certain aspects of it. Aretha Franklin made an album for the movie," Ember explained.

"Well, I've seen Harlem Nights already and there's a chance we'll be seeing it tomorrow anyway, so queue up Sparkle. Let me see what you're making such a fuss about."

"Really? Oh you won't regret it. It's cinematic magnificence. I promise." Cole wasn't so sure about that, but he loved to see Ember excited and he wanted to see her favorite movie. She hit the play button and snuggled back against him. He wrapped his arms around her and settled in to see what the fuss was about.

An hour and a half later Cole had to admit that Sparkle was all that Ember had hyped it up to be. At first he had been skeptical because most movies from the 70's were part of the Blaxploitation era and he wasn't a fan of those movies but that wasn't the case here. And while there were definite elements of chick flick, there was also enough other stuff to keep him interested.

Ember turned and looked up at him. "What did you think?"

"I think Stix is a damn good man, Sparkle has a beautiful voice, and I want to choke Satin Struthers for getting Sister hooked on that mess. Damn good movie. Thanks for getting me to watch it."

"I knew you were going to love it! What was your favorite part?"

"Honestly? The scene where they are in those dresses and singing that Something He Can Feel song. Now I see where En Vogue got the inspiration for their old video. Sexy doesn't even begin to describe that part. That's a man answer, right? I was supposed to say the church scene or something, huh?" he asked.

"Nope, that was exactly the right answer," Ember replied with mischief in her eyes. "Do me a favor and go sit in that chair over there. Face it towards that open space over there. I'll be right back." And then she grabbed her phone and disappeared into the bathroom.

Cole wondered what Ember was up to but he complied with her request. Little did he know that Ember had been practicing for this moment for years. Long ago she had created a sexy dance to that song. It was not for any reason in particular other than she found the song to be incredibly sexy, just like Cole had said. Years of practice in various full length mirrors and the fact that she had the song in her music folder on her phone brought her to the point where she was going to give Cole something he could feel, so to speak. She quickly stripped down to her purple bra and panty set and queued up the song on her phone.

"Are you ready?" she called through the bathroom door.

"Absolutely. I'm not sure what for but I'm ready for anything," Cole called back.

Ember hit play and emerged from the bathroom. The moment Cole saw her, his body reacted. White hot heat spread through him and the hair on his arms stood up. Ember was an enchantress in purple panties. She began to move her body to the music, swaying, turning, and bending over. Watching her was the sweetest torture. He wanted so badly to touch her but he didn't want the show to end. He burned this moment in his memory so that he could refer back to it when they were no longer together. His eyes followed her as she danced toward him. The closer she got, the harder he got. She stopped right in front of him and continued to sway to the music. She turned around, facing away from him and began to twerk. Cole felt like he was coming out of his skin.

"Take off your clothes," Ember requested as she continued to dance.

"What?" Cole asked. He wasn't sure he could move, let alone undress.

"Your clothes. Take. Them. Off. Now," she requested again. This time she gave him a visual as she reached around and unsnapped her bra, letting it slide down her arms and to the floor. Cole mimicked her actions and removed his tee shirt. Ember then slid her panties down her legs and stepped out of them. Again Cole followed suit and stood briefly to slide his sweats and boxer briefs down his legs before reclaiming his seat. The song was almost over and Ember joined Cole at the chair for her finale. She stood over him, placed her arms on his shoulders, and swayed her hips to the music as she lowered herself onto his lap. Just as the music ended, she sealed their bodies together and they began a rhythm of their own. She rode him, picking up the pace until he felt her pulse around him in orgasm. He followed behind her shortly and they remained on the chair for a few moments as they caught their breath. No words were said because none were needed.

Sometime a short while later Cole heard Ember stifle a yawn. He stood and carried her to the bed. He laid her down and then slid in beside her. Just as she drifted to sleep, he kissed her forehead and said, "Thank you."

Chapter Twenty-Four

"I think I'm getting used to sleeping in. I did not want to get up this morning," Cole announced during breakfast. It was day four of the cruise and they were sitting on the sun deck drinking coffee and eating the best French toast Cole had ever tasted.

"I know what you mean. But at least we won't die from heat exhaustion today. The boat docks at 7:30 so we have about 15 more minutes to eat and then we can go exploring around Grand Turk." Ember sounded excited.

"So, did you ever dance professionally? You were amazing last night," Cole asked, abruptly changing the subject and catching Ember completely off guard. "Wait, what did I do? Why are you looking at me like that?!"

Ember's face was flaming red with a look of pure shock. "You just asked me if I used to be a stripper! How should I look at you?"

"No no no! Not a stripper! A dancer! Like on a dance team. You went to an HBCU. They are known for dance troupes and modeling troupes. You know how to salsa and then last night . . ." Cole trailed off, trying to find the right words.

The look on his face was enough to dissolve Ember's flash of anger into laughter as he floundered for words. "Sorry, I jumped to conclusions. And not that there's anything wrong with being a stripper. I know quite a few women who stripped their way through college and came out with no loans." She wasn't going to disclose that Cheyenne had been one of those girls for a while.

"So . . . were you in a dance troupe in college?" Cole asked and ducked, acting like he was worried she would hit him.

"No and you're safe," she laughed. "In college my head was in the books. If it didn't have to do with academics, I was not involved. So there was no dance troupe or anything like that. I think I would have been terrified to dance in front of a large group of people. And Gabriella taught me how to salsa dance a long time ago. I've been salsa dancing quite a few times but until the other night it had been a while," she explained.

"Well . . . your talent is limitless. At least in my book," he commented with a smile that sent shivers down her back.

"Thank you." was her only reply.

"You two are trying to beat the heat today, huh?" Warren said, interrupting their conversation at just the right time. They had been so engrossed in each other, they hadn't noticed him walk up.

"That we are. I think I nearly died from heat exhaustion yesterday," Ember remarked. "Care to join us?"

"Maybe just for a moment. I have a meeting with ship security in a half hour or so but I could use some coffee." Warren signaled the waitress as he sat down. "Now wait a minute. How were you nearly dying from heat exhaustion when I distinctly remember you saying you were from Florida, Ember?"

"Now that is a good question," Cole agreed.

"Simple: I hate heat. And the heat in Florida is a type of disrespectful, invade your personal space, make you hate life

146

heat. I stayed inside most of the time growing up and then got out of there as soon as I could. That was eight years ago. Now that my parents have passed on, there's no reason for me to go back. And I won't because I don't like being disrespected."

Both men laughed at Ember's explanation. "That's actually a pretty accurate description of the heat in the Caribbean as well. I've gotten used to it though, so I no longer feel disrespected," Warren remarked.

"What should we look for on Grand Turk? We plan to visit the beach, of course, but do you recommend anything else?" Cole asked.

"Grand Turk used to be a huge part of the sea salt industry. There are Salinas on the island that date back as far as the 1700s. The Salt House museum has a lot of information on the history, development, and decline of the industry. I went to see it and I enjoyed it. There's also Her Majesty's Prison. It was, of course, a prison at one point but now it is a sort of museum on local crime and punishment. Very interesting exhibits," Warren explained.

"Is the prison haunted?" Ember asked.

Warren chuckled. "Not that I've ever heard of but it is very old. I think it was built in the early 1800s. So I imagine at least a few people have died there. Must be a few ghosts roaming around, right?"

"Maybe. Do you want to check out the prison Cole?" Ember asked.

"Because we're looking for ghosts?"

"Well, not looking but it would be cool to see one."

"Cool where? I'm good," Cole assured her.

"You're not scared, are you?" Warren asked, knowing full well the answer.

"No. But I'm not inviting trouble. Who goes somewhere and says 'Hey angry spirit that hasn't crossed over, let me bother you'? Nope, I'm good."

Ember and Warren dissolved into laugher while Cole held his ground. The trio talked about the island for a few more minutes. In the end, Cole and Ember decided to rent bicycles and ride to The Salt House and then visit the beach for a little while. As he and Ember gathered their things to head out to the island, something made Cole glance to the far left of where they were sitting. He caught sight of Vinny and Allen sitting at a table presumably eating breakfast. Vinny was staring directly at him and his expression was neither pleased nor friendly.

* * *

Ember and Cole enjoyed their time on Grand Turk Island. They relaxed on the beach for a while before it got too hot. Ember had worn a more modest but still sexy one-piece bathing suit so Cole managed to keep his hands to himself. Barely, but he managed it. When they left the beach they rented bikes and visited The Salt House. Ember even talked Cole into briefly stopping by the prison on their way to grab lunch. When they returned to the ship they both decided a nap was in order and slept until it was time for the movie marathon.

The movie theater was set up similar to a dinner theater for plays. There were tables with floor length black tablecloths and cushioned chairs. At the front was the movie screen; it was surrounded by burgundy curtains and had a vintage feel to it. The atmosphere was comfortable with a touch of sophistication. Ember led Cole to a table in the far back corner.

"Why all the way back here?" he asked.

"I don't like being up on everyone else. I don't go to movies much anymore but when I did, I would always go to the very far back and sit as far away from people as possible. Cheyenne, Gab, and Violet always got so annoyed with me" she explained. "They complained about having to go on a hiking expedition just to see a movie but they never disputed that the seats were indeed the best."

"I don't really have a preference, so the back is fine with me," Cole said.

Shortly after they sat down, a waitress arrived to take their order. After she took their order, she informed them that the movie marathon would include Harlem Nights, Cooley High, and The Five Heartbeats.

"See I told you Harlem Nights was going to be part of the marathon. You can't have a black movie marathon without an Eddie Murphy movie and Harlem Nights is the best Eddie Murphy movie," Cole explained.

"Better than Coming to America?" Ember asked.

"Come on, he shot off her pinky toe!" Cole replied and Ember fell out laughing.

"I love Cooley High but they could have done better than The Five Heartbeats," Ember said.

"What's better than The Five Heartbeats? It's a classic."

"The Temptations, The Jacksons, House Party . . ."

"House Party? You're pushing it with that one," Cole said as the curtains pulled back and the marathon started.

They ate, drank, and enjoyed themselves. Then, about half-way through The Five Heartbeats, Ember became restless. She never really cared for the movie, though she did love the soundtrack.

"There's another reason why it's good to sit all the way in the back in a dark movie theater," Ember whispered in Cole's ear as she slid her hand up his thigh and placed it on his crotch. He angled his head to look at her and she gave him a naughty wink.

He turned to whisper in her ear, "Remember the other day when you mentioned fantasies?" She nodded her head to indicate she did. "Well, uh, this is kind of mine. Making out in a movie theater. I know it's kind of high schoolish, but well . . . uh . . . you know," he faltered as Ember's hand became very busy undoing his zipper.

"Shhh, I'm trying to hear the movie," she whispered as she pulled his shaft out of his pants and began to stoke it. He couldn't have spoken at that moment if his life depended on it. Ember moved her hand up and down until he was rock hard and she could hear his labored breathing.

They were pretty isolated but she discreetly looked around to make sure no one was paying them any attention. Satisfied that no one was looking their way, she agilely slid under the table. Hidden now by the darkness and black tablecloth, Ember quickly finished unbuckling Cole's pants and opened them so she would have better access to his manhood. She grasped the base and wasted no time sliding it into her mouth. Cole's body instantly went rigid and she was pretty sure he was fighting the urge to moan. She continued to work her mouth up and down on him, stopping for a few seconds to swirl her tongue around his head.

Cole clenched his fists on the table and tried to look as normal as possible as Ember sucked the life out of him. She stopped again to swirl her tongue and he nearly shouted. Her mouth was magical. He knew he wouldn't last much longer with her doing that but that was fine because she didn't need to disappear for too long; they didn't need to push their luck. Ember drew him into her mouth clear to the base and he swore he was touching the back of her throat. She swirled her tongue around his length and he resisted the urge to buck his hips. She did it a few more times and then his body exploded into a million pieces. He gripped the table as she continued to suck, milking him for all he had. When his moment of ecstasy subsided, he felt the warmth of her mouth leave him and she gently returned his manhood and clothing to their original places. She then quickly slid back up into her chair and took a drink of her wine.

She leaned over and whispered, "Oh look, it's Eddie King Jr." and Cole tried to stifle his laughter. He was unsuccessful.

Chapter Twenty-Five

The next morning Ember returned to her room after spending the night with Cole. The movie theater had just been a warm up and they had returned to his room and made love until the wee hours of the morning.

Made love?

Yes, that's exactly what she had been doing. Because she loved him. Ember sat down on her bed and then laid down on her back to stare at the ceiling. *What the hell am I going to do now?* she silently asked herself. At the moment she had no answer and there wasn't a chance in hell that she was going to call Cheyenne or Gabriella. Gabriella would tell her something crazy about following her heart and she could just hear Cheyenne now: "Well who told your ass to go and catch feelings?!" Neither response was what she needed. At this point all she could do was think and try to formulate a plan. At least she had a little time and space away from Cole to figure out what she was going to do, since she only had two days before the cruise was over. After that her time with Cole would be over.

Today was a fun day at sea and Ember had a full day of beauty planned to get ready for the captain's dinner that night. First she had a massage, then a full body spa skin treatment and facial, followed by a full beauty package at the salon. She needed to take a shower, decide which dress to wear, choose a hairstyle that complimented the dress, and then head out for her massage appointment.

But all she could think about was Cole and what she would do when it all came to an end. Ember knew she couldn't go back to just being Cole's employee, so returning to Commercial Innovations was out of the question. She could not and would not go to work day in and day out having to face the man she loved knowing he would never love her in return. That would be absolute torture. That really only left her one other choice. Once they docked she would submit her formal resignation. She would take a few weeks of downtime to get over Cole and then she would begin establishing her own company. Maybe she would leave North Carolina. She was serious about never returning to Florida but Virginia or Maryland wouldn't be too far away from Cheyenne and Gabriella and she wouldn't have to worry about running into Cole.

Ember looked at the clock on her phone and decided that she would take a few minutes to think about a tentative plan now, that way she could relax and enjoy her day of beauty. She began to calculate in her head how much she would need to cover six months of living expenses and what she could budget for renting a space, building a website, trademarking a name and logo, advertising, and hiring at least an administrative assistant. The numbers started to get jumbled in her head, so she went to the table, sat down, grabbed her notebook, and began to jot down a rough outline of everything she was thinking. Ten minutes later she took a look at all she had written down. Though her plans were in their infancy, she knew achieving her dream was going to become a reality. She smiled but in the back of her mind she wished that she could share this joy with Cole. She shook her head as if to dismiss the thought, and went to get ready for her massage appointment.

* * *

Cole was standing at the bar drinking an old fashioned and feeling fine in his Armani suit. Ember text him earlier to let him know that she was running late and would meet him in the ballroom rather than have him pick her up from her room. It was probably just as well; he didn't have the best track record when it came to her opening her door looking beautiful. He smiled remembering what happened when she opened the door wearing that swimsuit the other day. He missed Ember while she was doing all her spa activities but it had given him time to make some very big decisions. His mother always said that he should step out on faith but other than when he started Commercial Innovations, he'd never put it into practice until this afternoon. When he stepped out on faith with Commercial Innovations he had only had himself as a factor. This time he had to place his faith in Ember as well. He looked up to see Warren heading his way.

"Well frat, I must say you where that color well," Warren said, indicating the tie Cole was wearing.

"Now you know real men rock gold," Cole replied.

"Indeed. How was your day at sea? Where's Ember?" Warren inquired.

"She had an all day spa thing that ran late so she told me she would meet me up here. I spent the day on the phone with my lawyer."

Warren's eyebrow shot up. "Something wrong?"

"No, something is right. Ember is right. I decided to prove to her that she has nothing to lose if we continue our relationship."

"And how exactly does a lawyer factor into that?"

"I'm making her a partner in Commercial Innovations," Cole stated matter-of-factly.

"I'm sorry, what?" Warren asked, disbelief clouding his features.

"Hear me out, man. When Ember and I first discussed the terms of this affair, she stated that it would end when we left the ship because she had a lot to lose and she was at a disadvantage because she's my employee. She's absolutely right. If I make her a partner, she is no longer at a disadvantage. We are equals and the state of our personal relationship becomes a non-factor. She's protected."

"But *you* aren't Cole. What are you doing to protect yourself? You're giving her half of your livelihood."

"Technically it's 49%. I kept 51% as the founding partner. And Commercial Innovations isn't my only business or source of income. Actually, it's not even my largest source of income anymore. I created it and I love it, but I love her more. Listen, my parents have been married for four solid decades. If you ask my dad how he knew my mom was for him, his answer is simple: he knew. I made a huge mistake with Denise. I didn't know; I assumed. I was wrong. I know with Ember."

"But you said she didn't even want to get married. Not now, not ever. You're going to give half of your life to someone who won't even be your wife. You have to see how ludicrous that is!"

"I'll take her anyway that I can have her," Cole responded truthfully.

"There's no talking you out of this?"

"No. I'm going to tell her tonight after dinner."

"Well, don't look now but your lady just walked in and she is turning heads," Warren advised him.

Cole turned and saw Ember walking towards them. She outshone every woman in the room. Her gown was strapless and dark blue with an empire waist. Golden crystals decorated the bodice and she wore matching gold arm-length gloves. Her strappy heels were also gold, as was the flower pinned behind her hair, which had been straightened and pinned in curls all over her head. She looked like a retro movie star and Cole was in awe of her beauty.

"Mind if I stand with the two best dressed men in here?" Ember asked when she reached Cole and Warren.

"That's quite a compliment coming from the most beautiful woman here tonight," Cole replied.

"You do indeed look amazing Ember," Warren complimented her. "Would you two mind me joining you tonight? Honestly, I usually sit the dinner out because I'm not one for much pomp and circumstance but tonight is the first of many surprise guest entertainers we will be featuring. The one scheduled for tonight is one of my favorite artists and I couldn't miss it."

"You can absolutely join us . . . if you give us a hint of who will be performing," Ember said.

"You drive a hard bargain, but here's a hint: she's from Philly and her name rhymes with her home," Warren said with a wink.

"Oh you can definitely sit with us," Ember said with an excited clap.

The evening was amazing but for Ember the most memorable part was swaying in Cole's arms while listening to the live performance. She committed that moment to memory. It was all she would have left in a few days.

Chapter Twenty-Six

Cole and Ember returned to her room just before midnight. Ember's feet were killing her but she wanted to wash the make up and spa lotion off so she stepped into the bathroom to take a quick shower. Cole sat down and began to undress. He stretched and laid back. He was a bit nervous about telling her that he was giving her half of his business but he hoped that she understood why he wanted to do it. And most of all he hoped that she would accept it. He could not imagine his world without her.

God, she had looked amazing tonight. For a brief moment he wondered what she would look like in a wedding dress. He knew it wasn't what she wanted but he would marry her in a minute. They could get married right here on this ship. His family would love to take a vacation like this and he was sure Cheyenne and Gabriella would love it too. He wondered if anyone was getting married on this particular cruise. His advertising mind kicked in as he realized that the wedding market could be a huge selling point for Soul Escapes. The ship had full suites, adjoining suites, a full spa, a beauty salon, and several areas that would be perfect for weddings of all sizes. He needed to write all of this down so he and Ember could go over it the next day.

Cole got up and grabbed Ember's notebook off of the table, intent on writing his ideas down. He flipped open the pages, looking for a blank sheet when his eye caught a page full of numbers. He knew they weren't his business but he looked anyway. As he read, anger filled his body when he realized that he was reading Ember's plans to start her own business. He slammed the book down, coming to the conclusion that he was being played for a fool. There was no way Ember could afford the numbers on this page on her own. She had to be planning to get it from him. It was Denise all over again. How could he be so stupid?! He got dressed and was just about to put his shoes on when he heard the shower stop and saw Ember emerge from the bathroom wrapped in a towel.

"So do you want to explain this to me?" Cole said grabbing the book from the table and holding it up for Ember to see.

"Why do you have that?" Ember asked, startled by his tone.

"I think the better question is why do you have detailed notes, including sums of money needed, about you starting your own company? Where are you getting this money? That's what this was all about, wasn't it? You screw me and then you *screw* me? Take my money, my company secrets, start your own company and become my damn competition?" Cole's voice was low and angry.

Ember couldn't believe her ears. "I don't need or want your money! You don't know what the hell you are talking about. And you went through my stuff. How dare you!"

"How dare me? You got a lot of fucking nerve! How else would you get the amount of money you have written here? Of course you were sleeping with me to get it. And what's sad is I would have given it to you! You had me hook, line, and sinker! I can't believe I almost let it happen again." He looked like he was about to explode. "Shit!"

"Get out! You don't know what I have or what I plan to do with it! I don't need you or want you! You're calling me a prostitute, accusing me of sleeping with you for money!"

"If the shoe fits, wear that shit," Cole said as he grabbed his shoes and strode purposely to the door. "You're fired." He threw back at her as he walked out of the door and slammed it behind him.

Ember sat on the edge of the bed trying to digest what just happened. She walked in the bathroom and everything was fine. She walked out to a shit storm. Why was Cole reading her notebook? How could he actually believe that she would use him for money? And what the hell was he talking about letting it happen again? She never received more than the paycheck she earned from him. She felt tears behind her eyes. This is why she didn't do love. It hurt too much.

She stood up and began to dress, pushing the tears back. She would not cry over this, she decided as she slipped into her shorts and pulled a tank top over her head. Luckily she was already prepared to leave Commercial Innovations and Cole. This wasn't the way she thought it would end but she had gained clarity along with her broken heart. Now she knew that she needed to be far away from him and his accusations. And she needed a drink. She grabbed her wallet, slipped on her sandals, and headed upstairs to get a glass of wine. Make that a couple of glasses.

* * *

Ember sat at a table at the far end of the bar hoping that would dissuade any friendly travelers from trying to engage her in conversation. A waitress came over and she ordered a glass of moscato. She probably could have used something a bit stronger but wine would have to do. The waitress returned in record time and Ember drank the contents of her glass even faster. She signaled for another and then stared at the stem of her glass. She silently fumed, angry at herself for falling in love with someone like Cole. He turned out to be just like all the other men she had encountered: cold, egotistical and self-serving. How dare he think that she needed to use him for anything? She had everything she could ever need and more and no man had given it to her for in exchange for sexual favors. After the time they spent together, how could he even think for one second that she was the type of woman who would even exchange sex for money? She knew he wasn't in love with her but for him to think such a thing, he couldn't even like her. She wanted so badly to call Cheyenne and Gabriella but she had another full day on the ship and she didn't want them to call her and worry her checking to see if she was okay. She wanted to spend the next twenty-four hours in her room, preferably sleeping, before she had to return to the real world. She also had absolutely no desire to run into Cole. He did her a solid by firing her. She would avoid him on the ship and send someone to gather her things from her office. If she had it her way, she would never see Cole again—though the thought brought tears to her eyes.

Ember was so lost in her anger that she didn't notice she had company until she heard a voice. "Need a refill?"

Ember looked up to see the next to last person she wanted to see. Vinny. The only way the company could have been worse was if it was Cole. He was holding a glass of wine in one hand and a mixed drink in the other. "I saw you request another drink from the waitress. I got it from her and brought it over. My treat," he offered.

"Thank you Vinny, but I can't accept. I'm honestly not in the mood for company. It would be rude for me to take the drink," Ember replied.

"Not rude at all. You can accept the drink and I will take my leave. I hope whatever is bothering you gets better," he said and then sat the glass of wine down and retreated to a table halfway across the room. Ember saw him take out a small notebook and begin to write something down.

Satisfied that Vinny wasn't going to request her attention any further, she began to drink the gifted glass of wine. She decided this would be her last drink for the night. She was a lightweight and didn't want to get drunk. She also didn't want to give Vinny the opportunity to come back attempt conversation again.

She thought about how the last two weeks had been the craziest time of her adult life. How had Cole gone from her boss, to her lover, to the love of her life, to the person who hurt her the most in such a short time frame? Tears clouded her eyes again and blurred her vision as she tossed back the rest of the wine and set her glass down. She wiped the tears away but the blurred vision remained. She wiped her eyes again and instantly felt dizzy. She tried wiping her eyes again but couldn't quite get her arms to her face. They felt like they weighed 1000 pounds. She heard a familiar voice but couldn't quite make out the words and then she was standing. She thought she was walking—maybe floating. She had no idea. The last thing she remembered was walking into a wall before everything went black.

Chapter Twenty-Seven

"You're going to have to go talk to her. You don't know the whole story," Warren told Cole.

"I know the whole damn story. It's the story of my life. Boy meets girl. Boy stupidly falls in love. Girl attempts to use boy. Boy gets hurt. Girl moves on to the next fool. Wash. Rinse. Repeat." Cole said and took a gulp of his whiskey.

"You don't know the whole story, you just assume you know it and in typical Scotch Bonnet style, you flipped before making sure you had something to flip about."

"How are you suddenly on her side? A few hours ago you thought I was a fool for wanting to make her a partner. Now I'm a fool for not trusting her? Make up your damn mind man," Cole requested angrily.

"That's my point exactly. A few hours ago you were 100% ready to sign over half of a business you built from the ground up to Ember. You trusted her that much. Don't you think you should give her the benefit of the doubt to at least find out her side? You said that she denied that she wanted money from you. Maybe there's something you don't know."

"Of course she denied it. She had been caught."

"But if she had only been in it for the money and the jig was up, why would she still deny it?" Warren asked.

"How should I know? Maybe she thought she could trick me again. Deceitful people do crazy things."

"And hurt people hurt people. You love her and she hurt you. Instead of finding out all the facts, you hurt her back," Warren countered.

The two men lapsed into silence. Warren thought about ways to help his friend and Cole silently wished he could go back two hours and never pick up Ember's book. Cole also silently acknowledged that Warren could have a point and he probably did need to talk to Ember. It wouldn't be tonight though.

A knock on the door interrupted the silence and Cole muttered, "I sincerely hope that isn't Vinny the Dick." Warren shared the sentiment but chose not to comment as he stood to go answer the door. He opened it to find a member of his security team.

"What wrong?" he asked. He knew there was a problem if security was knocking on his door at nearly 2am.

"We have a situation sir. Can I come in?"

"Yes, of course. Now tell me what's going on."

"We think we may have a date rape drug situation on our hands. One of our bartenders, Gayle, witnessed a man give a woman a glass of wine. She noticed because the man actually took the glass from a waitress who was on her way to deliver it to the woman, paid for it, and then took it over to his own table before getting back up and then giving it to the woman. Gayle looked away for a while but noticed that the man had gone back to his own table. When she looked up again the man and woman were walking out but Gayle claims the woman looked groggy so she radioed me and told me over the phone while I headed over here to alert you. They left less than 10 minutes ago. Also strange is that the woman let her wallet. One of the waitresses is bringing it to me right now. She said the name on the ID inside was Amber something. She didn't know the man's name and he paid in cash so there's no receipt but she can describe him. She said he was flashy and very memorable." There was a knock on the door and Warren opened it. A waitress was on the other side and handed the security man the wallet then left. As Warren closed the door the man opened the wallet and said the name out loud. "Ember Sinclair. Her room key is in here--"

"What the fuck?!"

"Shit!"

Both Cole and Warren exclaimed at the same time startling the security man. Cole jumped up and stood in front of him. "Give me that!" he demanded.

The security man looked to Warren and Warren exclaimed "Give it to him!" The man complied and Cole snatched the ID. It was indeed Ember's.

"You said the waitress said the man was flashy?" Cole asked.

"Yes sir."

"It's got to be that fuck Vinny," Cole said to Warren as he ran for the door. "What room is he in?!

Warren was right on Cole's heels. "He's on the same floor as you but on the other side. Cabin 115," he shouted as they ran. "Turn and take the stairs. That's faster than the elevator. Go!"

* * *

I'm going to thoroughly enjoy this, Vinny thought to himself as he tugged Ember's shorts and underwear down her legs. Not only was he about to have the woman he wanted since he first laid eyes on her the other day but he was also going to take something that belonged to Cole Bainbridge. He didn't believe it for a second when they claimed they were just boss and employee and then he knew for certain that they were lying when they kissed at the pool. Vinny had heard of hot shot Cole Bainbridge long before they met on the ship. You couldn't be black in the ad industry and not at least know of him. In fact, Foster Glenn had lost more than one account to Commercial Innovations over the years.

Vinny yanked off Ember's tank top and reached around to remove her bra. He paused for a moment to look at her naked body. *Oh, this is going to be so good*, he assured himself. He swore he had the best luck. He had almost stayed in his room tonight but decided that he needed some female attention. He had planned to find some lonely woman abandoned by her friends and get her back to his room. Just in case he couldn't find anyone willing, he had packed a little security in his pocket in the form of a rohpy. Imagine his surprise to see Ember, without Cole, drinking alone and looking upset. Perfect timing, perfect opportunity, and perfect revenge. He would get to screw Ember, she wouldn't remember a thing except waking up in bed with him, and that would ruin whatever it was that Cole and Ember had because Cole was the type of man that did not share. That Vinny was sure of.

Vinny took off his shirt and shorts and then slid his boxers down. He was about to join Ember on the bed when there was a knock at his door. He stood stock-still, not making a sound, hoping that whomever it was would think he wasn't there and leave. The knock came again and then he heard someone shout, "Fuck this knocking shit," seconds before the heavy door swung open and Cole ran in.

Cole took one look at Ember's naked, unconscious form and ran up on Vinny swinging. Punch after punch landed on every part of Vinny's body. He tried to fight back but Cole was fueled by a deadly combination of fear and anger. Before long Vinny slumped to the floor, unconscious. That didn't stop Cole and he seemed intent on killing him. Warren had to wrestle Cole to the ground, catching a few jabs himself, so that the rest of security could detain Vinny's unconscious form. Now a little calmer, Cole looked up at Ember and noticed that someone, probably security, had covered her with the blanket from the bed. He sent up a prayer that he had been in time and Vinny hadn't touched her other than undressing her. He got up and attempted to redress her but a member of security stopped him.

"I'm sorry sir, but we have to treat this as a crime scene and take pictures so charges can be filed. We also need to have the ship physician examine Ms. Sinclair before she can be dressed or moved," the man explained.

Cole wanted to argue but he knew the man was right. So he sat down on the floor in front of the bed, because he wasn't leaving her again, and waited.

Chapter Twenty-Eight

Cole was exhausted but he knew there was no way he was going to go to sleep anytime soon. He was back in his cabin sitting in the chair watching Ember as she slept off the effect of the rohypnol Vinny had given her. As soon as the crime scene had been cleared and the doctor had examined her, Cole dressed her in her shorts and tank top and then carried her back to his room. She had been released into his care because the doctor had determined that it had been an attempted rape, not a successful one.

His anger began to rise again when he thought of what almost happened. Warren was right; he should have never walked out on her without discussing what he'd found in her notebook. Now that he had time to think about the situation, he was pretty sure there had to be a logical explanation. Ember wouldn't use him; he knew that. But honestly, even if she was trying to get money out of him, she could have it. Hell, she could have it all, as long as she stayed in his life. He loved her that much. There was a soft knock at the door. Cole wearily rose and opened the door to see Warren standing on the other side. He motioned for him to enter.

"She's still out, huh?" Warren asked.

"The doctor said the effects of rohypnol can last up to eight hours. He estimated that Ember ingested it around 1:45am so she could be out until roughly 10am. And even after she comes to she could be drowsy and lethargic," Cole explained.

"I hate that this happened to her. I'm so sorry man."

"It's not your fault. If anyone is guilty, it's me. I walked out on her. She would have never been at the bar drinking alone if I hadn't walked out on her," Cole said.

"You can't do that to yourself Cole. The only one at fault in this situation is that piece of shit Vinny. There's no way that you could have known he would pull something like this. The FBI has been alerted and the Coast Guard is transporting agents to the ship as we speak."

"The FBI?"

"Standard practice for crimes committed at sea. Vinny is in a holding cell in the ship's bowel. He came to a while ago and asked for pain medication. He's still waiting," Warren said. "You should try to get some rest. The sun will be up soon and Ember will wake up. There's no telling how she's going to handle this and you need to be there for her."

"You're right but I'm not sure I can sleep right now. I will try though," Cole promised as he and Warren walked to the door.

"I'll let you know when the FBI comes aboard. They are going to have to talk to Ember. We shouldn't have to dock, so they will most likely come to the room to interview her. Knowing that she was drugged, I doubt that they will make her get up and move elsewhere to talk."

"Okay, thank you. I appreciate everything, man."

"No problem," Warren said as he walked through the door. Cole closed the door and sat back down at the table. He put his feet up on the other chair and tilted his head back. He was asleep moments later.

* * *

Cole's phone buzzed in his pocket, startling him awake. He noticed that the sun had come up as he retrieved the phone from his pocket and saw Rock's name scrolling across the top. The clock said 6:32am.

He turned to face away from Ember so his voice didn't disturb her. "Is everything okay?" Cole asked. He didn't think he could take anymore emergencies today.

"Yes, I just wanted to catch you when I thought you would be alone. Can you talk?"

"Yeah. I'm just waiting for the FBI to show up," Cole said groggily.

"The FBI? Why the hell are you waiting on the FBI Cole?" Rock demanded.

"It's a long story man."

"Then start from the beginning and start now," Rock demanded.

Cole literally went to the beginning, when he and Ember first agreed to their affair and told Rock everything, including the argument they had last night before the attempted rape.

"Jesus, Cole. What is wrong with people? Is Ember okay mentally? This has to be hard on her."

"She's still out cold and could be until around 10," Cole explained.

"And where is that piece of shit that tried to rape her?

"Apparently all cruise ships come equipped with a holding cell in the bowel of the ship. He's down there until the FBI arrives. According to Warren he was pretty banged up."

"He's lucky he's alive with what he tried to pull. I wish I was there to help. I can't do much from here but I can tell you that I did some background checking on Ember. I know you only asked me about Violet but I could tell you were getting in deep with Ember and I wanted to check her out."

"Dammit Rock, that's not what I asked you to do," Cole said, unaware that a pair of eyes was now watching him.

"Yes, I know. But what I found out will help you understand what that list you found in her notebook was about and will ease your mind about her trying to use you."

"I've already let that go man. She can have whatever she wants. I just need her near me. She can bleed me dry. I don't care."

"Cole, she won't bleed you dry. She'd have to bleed herself dry first and that could prove to be very difficult."

"I don't get it," Cole replied.

"Ember is rich. Not new money rich but old, family money rich. Well, actually she's the best of both worlds. Her mother is, or rather was, Elizabeth Foster."

"The writer? That Elizabeth Foster?!"

"Yes, and when she died Ember became the soul heir of all her royalties and unpublished manuscripts. Rumor has it that Ms. Foster left over 20 full manuscripts and the outlines of at least 30 more books. The fact that they are published posthumously only adds to their popularity and value. With this alone Ember would never have to work again if she didn't want to. But there's more," Rock advised.

"I don't think I can take much more, man."

"Well, take a deep breath because here it comes. Ember's father, Jack Sinclair, was part of one of the richest families in Florida. They own massive amounts of real estate. When he died not only did he leave her an obscene amount of money, but she took his place on the board for the umbrella company that oversees all of the Sinclair family real estate holdings.

She's a silent board member but the money she rakes in is quite loud, big brother."

"Holy fucking shit."

"Right. Ember is sitting on enough money that she could loan you some, buy a couple of houses, own a basketball team, fund some aspiring rappers, buy a mall, and still not make a dent in her back account," Rock joked.

"But then why does she work for me? If she has all the money you claim she does, why didn't she start her own business right after college if that's what she wanted?" Cole asked, genuinely confused.

"Because I had a plan," Cole heard a weak voice reply from behind him. He spun around to see Ember staring at him with tired but alert eyes.

"Rock, I have to go," Cole said quickly. He hit the off button and quickly closed the difference between him and the bed and sat down on the edge. "How are you feeling?"

"Like I walked into a fog and stayed there for a few years. Why would you let me bleed you dry?" she asked as she struggled to sit up.

"No, the doctor said you need to stay still," Cole said as he gently put his hand on her shoulder to prevent her from rising. "Do you remember anything from last night?" Cole asked.

"I don't want to talk about last night. Right now I want to know why you would tell your brother that you would let me bleed you dry. Why would you give me all of your money? And don't say because you know I have my own. I was listening. You didn't know about my money when you said that."

"You heard that, huh?"

"Every word. Now tell me why."

Cole stood up and ran his hand down his face. "Look, I know you don't love me but I love you. You can have whatever you want, not that you need anything from me. I think you have feelings for me, even if you don't love me. Stay with me. I love you enough for the both of us. I know you don't believe in marriage. You don't have to marry me. Just . . . just stay with me. Please." Cole stared into her eyes and saw pools of tears appear. "Don't cry. Shit, I'm sorry I even brought this up right now. You went through so much last night. We don't have to talk about this now. Please don't cry," he pleaded as he sat down next to her and wiped away the tears that were now spilling down her cheeks.

"You don't understand Cole, these are happy tears. That list you found, I made it because I couldn't continue to work with you. I couldn't go to work day in and day out and see you."

"How is that happy? You couldn't stand to be around me?" Cole asked, confused.

"Because I couldn't stand to be around the man I loved knowing that he didn't love me back. I had to get away," Ember explained.

Realization hit Cole like a ton of bricks. "You love me?!"

"With my whole and entire heart," Ember responded.

Cole leaned in and placed a gentle kiss on Ember's lips. As he was pulling away, there was a knock on the door. "That must be the FBI."

"FBI?" Ember asked.

Cole opened the door but he didn't find the FBI, instead he found a ship employee holding a small stack of papers.

"Cole Bainbridge?" he asked.

"Yes."

"These were faxed to you and flagged for immediate delivery," he handed Cole the papers and left.

Cole closed the door and began flipping through the papers, realizing that they were the forms he had his lawyer draw up yesterday giving Ember partnership in Commercial Innovations. God, that seemed so long ago but it had been less than twenty-four hours. So much had happened.

Ember slowly sat up in the bed and Cole sat next to her. He handed her the papers and let her look through them. When she realized what they were, her head snapped up and she stared at Cole in shock. "You want to give me half of your company?!"

"Yes. I was going to tell you last night when you got out of the shower. I would marry you in a minute but I know that's not what you want. So I thought that if I gave you half of Commercial Innovations you would feel secure enough in your job to stay with me. But then I saw your notebook and . . ."

"You were willing to do this, even though you thought I didn't love you back and I didn't want to get married? You love me that much?"

"Yes," Cole stated simply.

Ember's tear began to flow again. "Yes Cole," he said.

Confusion clouded his features. "Yes what?"

"Yes, I'll marry you."

Cole blinked, sure he'd heard her incorrectly. "You'll marry me?"

"Yes," Ember repeated.

"Now?! Today?!"

"If that's what you want. The sooner the better."

Cole jumped up and began to pace excitedly. "I had this thought of us getting married on this ship. I actually thought it was good enough to use it to market the cruiseline. I grabbed your notebook to write it down. That's how all of this even happened. Jesus." Cole sat down in the chair and let it all process.

"Cole?"

"Yes, sweetheart?"

"Why is the FBI on its way?" Ember asked.

"You don't remember anything from last night?"

"Yes, of course I do. I remember the captain's dinner. Our fight. I needed a drink so I went up to the bar and drank wine. Did I drink too much? Is that why I feel like this? Do I have a hangover? I've never had one before. I only remember drinking two glasses. Then nothing else."

"Ember, there's no easy way to say this so I'm going to just going to rip the bandage off. That shit ball Vinny drugged you and tried to rape you last night."

"What?!" Ember said and tried to jump out of the bed. Still woozy from the drug, she swayed and nearly fell but Cole was there to catch her. He lowered her back to the bed just as they heard a knock at the door.

"You stay put," he warned Ember who was now crying as the realization of last night's events caught up with her. Cole opened the door to see Warren with two very official looking individuals, a man and a woman, standing behind him.

The FBI had arrived.

Chapter Twenty-Nine

Cole watched Ember walk towards him and he was once again captivated by her beauty. She had on a pale gold floor length strapless gown that hugged her curves and took Cole's breath away. Her hair was piled on top of her head in a beautiful bun and she was wearing a small gold and crystal tiara. Warren jabbed him in the side and reminded him not to drool. He smiled as he thought about how strong Ember had been today. Though she had no memory of it, a horrible thing happened to her, yet she handled the questions from the FBI like a champ.

When the FBI left the ship they took Vinny and Allen with them and promised that Vinny would be prosecuted under South Carolina law in accordance with the Cruise Vessel Security and Safety Act of 2010. Ember would be needed to testify but it would most likely be an open and shut case. And after all of that, she still insisted they get married today. She claimed she wanted to walk off the ship as Mrs. Cole Bainbridge. God, that was music to his ears.

As the ship chaplain preformed the ceremony linking their lives together, Ember thought about how truly blessed she was and how wrong she had been about love. With the right person, love was everything. She hated that Gabriella and

Cheyenne weren't here with her but she knew they would understand. Eventually. The chaplain called for the rings and Ember saw Warren pass Cole a small bag. From it he produced two bands and a third ring. Tears clouded her eyes when she realized that the third ring was the amber and diamond ring she had fallen in love with in Nassau. She looked at Cole.

"I went back that day when you returned to the ship and got it. I was going to give it to you our last night on the ship," he explained.

"And now you are doing just that," she said through her tears. The chaplain pronounced them man and wife and Cole sealed their union with a kiss. It was the best moment of his life.

* * *

"Well, Mrs. Bainbridge, what's on your mind?" Cole asked later that night as he watched Ember stare out of the porthole in her cabin. They had returned there to spend their wedding night.

She smiled at the use of her new name and looked over at him. "Life is funny."

"It is."

"Care to elaborate?"

"You and I spent all that time running from love, only to run smack into each other. Just proves you can't hide from fate," she said as she stood and began to undress.

Cole moved behind her to unzip her gown. "No you can't. But maybe that was part of our fate, or rather our path. We had to deal with all of the unpleasantness, doubt, and fear to truly appreciate the amazing thing we have now," he explained as Ember's dress dropped to the floor. She turned and stood before him in a pale pink bra and panty set and thigh high stockings. He reached around her to unsnap her bra and stole a kiss on the way back. He then tugged her panties down and she stepped out of them. "The stockings stay," he requested.

Ember turned and made her way to the bed. Cole's manhood rose to stand at attention as he watched her butt bounce as she walked. "I'm trying to figure out why you still have on clothes," she said as she sat down to wait for him to disrobe.

Cole undressed in record time and joined Ember on the bed. He leaned in to push her back on the bed but she stopped him and changed their positions so he was laying on his back and she was hovering over him. She kissed her way down his chest and torso, hovering just above his shaft and then sealed her mouth around him. He bucked off the bed and snarled his hands in her hair as she alternated between deep heavy sucking and light teasing pulls. She continued for a few moments, until he pulled her head away and said, "If you keep this up . . ."

She obliged him and stopped, only to turn around and climb on his lap. Recognizing the position that Ember was moving into, Cole reached forward and guided her backwards, positioning her just over top of him. She eased down and slowly sealed their bodies together. Once he filled her completely, she began to ride him slowly. Because of the position, he reached new places as she moved up and down and moaned her pleasure. He reached up to grab her behind and rubbed his hands all over her.

She increased the pace and Cole began to flex upward to meet her downward movements. Faster and faster she rode until she felt the first of the spasms that indicated her orgasm was coming. Cole, close himself, sat up and wrapped his arms around her, sealing their bodies together just as Ember tumbled over the edge and took him with her. She felt him pulse inside of her as she closed tightly around him. They stayed that way as their breathing returned to normal. Eventually Cole lay back down and Ember disconnected their bodies, turned around, and laid down next to him.

"Thank you," she said.

"For what?" he asked.

"Cheyenne recently accused me of barely living and she was right. My fire was dead. Being with you reignited my flame and showed me I was missing out on life and love."

"So, I'm Ember's Flame?" he asked.

She chuckled, "Yes, you are. My forever flame."

Epilogue

Cheyenne and Gabriella were leaned up against Gabriella's car making small talk with Rock when they saw Cole and Ember walking towards them from the ship. When the couple reached the trio, they were smiling ear to ear as they reached to clasp hands. Rock's eyebrow immediately shot up and Gabriella eyed the couple curiously. Cheyenne was the first to speak.

"Why are you two grinning like fools and what's that about?" she said gesturing to their hands.

"We . . ." Cole began but Ember interrupted him.

"No, let me tell them," she said with a laugh.

"Somebody better say something," Cheyenne warned.

"Go ahead," Cole said, holding his grin.

"We got married yesterday evening."

"What?!" Cheyenne and Gabriella said in unison.

"Jesus! We sent you out to have a fling and you come back with a husband?! Who left the damn gate open?!" Cheyenne exclaimed.

"Saw that coming a mile away," Rock said as he moved to hug his brother and new sister-in-law.

"I bet you did," Cole chuckled, returning his hug.

"Well I didn't, and I want to know how this happened!" Gabrielle demanded.

"And we need to decide how she is going to pay for getting married without us!" Cheyenne added.

"We'll tell you the whole story. You want to head back over to that café and eat? I swear we will tell you everything. I wore the gold dress you picked out Gab and the shoes you picked out Chey, so you were there in spirit," Ember said, closing the distance between her two friends and hugging them.

"Actually, we have more pressing issues to discuss," Rock countered.

"What could be more pressing than this miracle marriage?" Cheyenne said, still hugging Ember and Gabriella.

"Cole, this is what I was calling to tell you yesterday morning but you hung up on me before I could finish." Rock looked at the three women. "Your friend Violet is alive. And she's in trouble."

And now . . .

A sneak peek at

Rocking

Cheyenne

Chapter One

Cheyenne Nighthorse stared at the man seated across from her and tried to focus on the words he was saying. It was hard because every emotion she could think of was coursing through her body all at once. Fear, disbelief, shock, elation, and white hot anger were waging a war inside of her and she honestly didn't know which one would be the victor. Violet was gone. She was dead. Cheyenne had accepted that fact and buried her, well mentally. You can't bury a body that you don't have. Yet here was Rock Bainbridge insisting that Violet was alive. Who the hell did he think he was?

Cheyenne looked over at her best friend Ember and saw tears streaming down her face. She was being comforted by her new husband, Cole. Cheyenne then looked to her left at her other best friend, Gabriella. She was squeezing the life out of her purse straps and looked as distraught as Ember. Cheyenne felt her anger grow. How dare he come and upset them this way? They should be celebrating Ember's surprise marriage, not revisiting Violet's tragic death. She slapped her hands down on the table, startling the already edgy group. All eyes were on her, something she hadn't quite anticipated, but she wouldn't waste the moment. "This is a bunch of speculation and bullshit. I'm out," she stated with a voice of steel and then slid out of the booth and quickly walked away.

"Totally saw that coming," Gabriella said, releasing her purse straps and wiping the tears from her eyes.

"I'm surprised she lasted this long," Ember admitted with a sigh.

"It's a rarity, but I'm confused. Why would finding out that your friend is alive make her angry?" Rock asked as he watched Cheyenne storm out of the front of the dinner and move toward the parking lot.

"Because Cheyenne is convinced that Violet is dead. I've been trying to tell her that she's still alive but for some reason she refused to even entertain the thought," Ember responded, slowly disengaging herself from Cole's embrace. "I'll go talk to her," she declared with a sigh as she stood up.

"This is going to be a two person job. I'm not sending you out there alone," Gabriella said solemnly as she stood up and followed Ember toward the exit.

Rock looked at his brother in complete disbelief. "What in the hell is wrong with that woman? I can think of 50 people right off hand that would kill to receive the news that their loved one is alive. She's a piece of work. What do you know about her?"

"She's not a suspect, Rock," Cole warned.

"Everyone is a suspect big brother." Rock retorted. "Tell me what you know."

"Honestly, not as much as you probably want me to. They are all best friends; Ember and Cheyenne grew up together in Florida. Apparently they couldn't wait to get out of there because they got themselves some scholarships, moved to North Carolina for college, and never looked back. They met Gabriella and Violet freshman year. Gabriella was attending the local cosmetology school and she did Ember and Cheyenne's hair and then joined them at the university their sophomore year. Violet was in one of Cheyenne's classes. They've been tight ever since. Ember did tell me that as much as she believed that Violet was still alive, Cheyenne equally believed Violet wasn't and they fought because of it. The beefs never last long, though. Ember just thinks that believing Violet is dead is Cheyenne's way of dealing with it," Cole explained.

"I need to talk to all three of them. Separately and then together. Do you think that's going to be a problem?" Rock asked.

"Uh . . ." Cole said as he glanced out the window and saw Cheyenne, Gabriella, and Ember in an obviously heated discussion complete with waving arms and tears.

Rock followed his line of vision. "Shit," he said, rubbing his hand down his face in agitation.

"Yeah, we need to come up with a game plan," Cole advised. "Let me make some calls while they're doing . . . that," he said gesturing towards the arguing women. "That way once they're done, we can set this plan in motion. I know you haven't had a chance to fully explain everything you found, but I imagine if you say Violet's in trouble time is of the essence," Cole said.

"Yes and no. Truthfully, if whoever has her wanted her dead, she would be dead by now. Too much time has passed. I have my theories, and one in particular that I'm leaning towards, but I need more information before I can figure out what our first, and subsequent, moves are. If one of my theories proves correct, and it's the one I'm banking on at this point, then Violet is not in any immediate danger and the way to get her out of the "trouble" she's in is to pursue outside sources, not directly look for her at this point. She could be— what?" Rock asked when he saw the aggravated look on his brother's face.

"Stop being so damn cryptic. I have no idea what you're even saying right now," Cole requested.

"Find us all a place to stay for a few days, preferably rooms next to each other. I have to be cryptic until I talk to them," Rock said, turning his attention back to the three women. They were still arguing and Cheyenne looked like she was ready to pounce. "Should we go out there and break it up?"

"I'm not going out there until we have somewhere to take them and something to feed them," Cole said as he grabbed his cell phone and began to search for suites in the area. "Unless you want to go out there and try to break that up with no where to go."

Rock watched as Cheyenne stomped her foot and Gabriella gave her the finger. "Nah, I'm good."

* * *

"Why won't you even entertain the fact that Violet is still alive?!" Ember demanded. They had been at it for at least ten minutes and she was quickly getting tired of arguing.

"Why are you so quick to believe a man you've only met once?" Cheyenne countered jabbing her pointer finger in Ember's direction.

"He's a PI, Cheyenne. It's not like he's an accountant with a hunch. This is what he does for a living," Gabriella interjected, hoping to calm everyone down with logic.

"Who says he's a good one? What do we know about him? Nothing except he's Cole's brother and only Ember knows Cole. I've seen him twice my whole life! I'm supposed to take the word of someone I hardly know, because someone I barely know knows my best friend? Hell no!" Cheyenne fired back.

"What the hell are you saying?! You're talking in a circle. Rock must be good because he found out all my business in a matter of days. There's your proof!" Ember explained.

"Wait what?" Gabriella asked Ember.

"Rock dug into my past when he saw that Cole was falling for me. He found about the money from mom and dad and told Cole. Cole had asked him to look into Violet's disappeared, but he looked me up too."

"See! He can't be trusted!" Cheyenne exclaimed, stomping her foot. "He's shady boots on the sly prying into people's lives and you want me to trust him?!

"This is not about you!" Gabriella yelled, shooting Cheyenne her middle finger. She turned back to Ember. "Rock did that? Cole married you after he knew you had money?" Gabriella asked, instantly concerned.

"No, no. He had already given me 49% percent of Commercial Innovations before he found out. He didn't marry me for my money, Gab," Ember explained, putting a reassuring arm around the woman she considered a sister. She knew why Gabriella was asking and wanted to make sure she understood that everything was kosher.

"You own half of Commercial Innovations?!" Gabriella exclaimed.

"Yes. Cole had the documents drawn up and faxed to us on the ship. And that was when he thought I was using him for his money."

"This is too much. I need you to tell me the whole story." Gabriella requested.

"See this, THIS, is what we should be doing right now. Not chasing a ghost," Cheyenne said. She immediately knew she had gone too far when she found herself staring into the eyes of a very angry Blactina.

"Just what the hell is wrong with you?! Why do you say stuff that you know will rile others up? That was completely uncalled for! You're not convinced? Fine. Then hear him out. Get all the facts and then form an educated opinion, because right now you're acting like a damn idiot. What if she is alive and we can help find her? Don't we owe her at least that? Get your head out of your ass!" Gabriella lit into her.

Before Cheyenne could respond Ember put her hand up, silencing her. "Gabriella is right. We owe it to Violet to at least see what Rock knows. I trust that he's good at what he does and we are going to find out what happened to Violet. Best case scenario, and what I think will happen, is we find her. Worst case scenario is that he leads us to her body and we'll finally have closure. I need one of these things to happen. I need to know. And I think you do too Chey, whether you want to admit it or not."

"I already know," Cheyenne insisted.

"You think you do. You convinced yourself you do. But you don't. If you won't do it for yourself, do it for Violet and us. Let us get the closure you think you have," Gabriella implored.

Cheyenne knew she could be a hard ass, but she would do anything for the women she considered sisters. "Fine. For y'all," she reluctantly agreed.

"It's a bonus that you get to look at Rock Bainbridge. I think you called him a gray-eyed walking wet dream, correct?" Gabriella offered.

"More like a gray-eyed devil. I don't trust him. I don't care how fine he is, he has a permanent spot on my shit list."

"He's really not that bad Chey. He looked into my background to protect his brother and I can respect that. He also kept Cole calm while I was unconscious. Apparently Cole was really messed up but I have no recollection," Ember explained.

"UNCONCIOUS?!" Cheyenne exclaimed. "Why the hell were you unconscious? Were you hurt?"

"No. I was almost raped," Ember replied.

"RAPED!" Cheyenne and Gabriella screamed and then began demanding answers at the same time. All three women began talking at the same time and no one could get a solid sentence out before someone was interrupting her.

"Ladies, how about we take this to a more suitable location?" Cole offered loudly, trying to make his voice heard over the mêlée. He clearly startled them because Ember and Gabriella jumped and Cheyenne rewarded him with an icy glare. "Sorry to startle you. I just think we need to go somewhere where we can stretch out and get everything out on the table. I've secured us a suite of rooms for the next few days. Ember and I can be away from work for a few more days. Rock is good to go. Cheyenne and Gabriella, can you take a few days off from work?"

"Yes we can." Gabriella answered quickly, shooting Cheyenne a look that clearly read keep your mouth closed.

"Good. I would love to drive you all over to our destination. Rock will follow in his truck." Cole explained in a soothing tone only a true southern gentleman could achieve. All three women nodded, though Cheyenne's nod was clearly reluctant, and he thanked his lucky stars that no one was putting up a fight. "Okay, let's head on out," he requested and they began making their way to Gabriella's car.

Cheyenne glanced behind her as she walked and saw Rock getting into a black Chevy Tahoe with dark tinted windows. She reluctantly admitted that he had to be the finest man she'd ever seen. Too bad she hated his guts.

Book Club Discussion Questions

1. Did it take time to get into reading the book or were you immediately drawn into the story? Why or why not?
2. What were your most and least favorite parts of Ember's Flame?
3. Did the characters seem authentic and believable in their roles?
4. What characters did you most and least relate to? Who are you most like?
5. What characters would you be friends with? Who would you dislike?
6. Does the new couple have a chance at lasting love or did they move too fast?
7. Do you see any other relationships forming in this book? If so, who?
8. Would you want to take a trip with Soul Escapes Cruise Line?
9. If you were making Ember's Flame into a movie, who would you cast as Ember and Cole?
10. Share a favorite quote from the book. Why did this quote stand out?
11. What feelings did Ember and Cole's story evoke in you?
12. How did Ember and Cole evolve and change throughout the story?
13. Was the story plot-driven or character-driven?

14. Did Ember's Flame seem realistic to you? Could it have happened in real life?
15. Did you notice any themes in the book?
16. Did the book change your perspective of anything? Why or why not?
17. If you could build a soundtrack for Ember's Flame, what three songs would you have to include?
18. Do Vinny's actions speak to a larger problem in society? Have you encountered a Vinny?
19. What do you think happened to Violet?
20. The author's slogan is "real love stories involve sex". How true or false do you find this?
21. Did you come away from this book wanting to read more by Serendipity?

The Soul Escapes Series

Join Serendipity on her blog for a **FREE** short story series based on the Soul Escapes Cruise Line that Ember and Cole fell in love on. A new story will be posted every month, beginning in September 2018. Check back monthly for a new story at www.authorserendipity.com.

Connect with the Author

Website: www.authorserendipity.com

Facebook: Author Serendipity

Instagram: authorserendipity

Twitter: AuthSerendipity

Email: author.serendipity@gmail.com

Creative Control With Self-Publishing

Divine Legacy Publishing provides authors with the guidance necessary to take creative control of their work through self-publishing. We provide:

Let Divine Legacy Publishing help you master the business of self-publishing.

Made in the USA
Columbia, SC
27 October 2020